Choosing To Love A Lady Thug 4

TN Jones

Choosing To Love A Lady Thug 4 © 2017 by TN Jones

All rights reserved. No part of this book may be reproduced in any form or by any electronic or mechanical means including information storage and retrieval systems, without permission in writing from the author. The only exception is by a reviewer, who may quote short excerpts in a review.

Cover designed by Bryant Sparks

This book is a work of fiction. Names, characters, places, and incidents either are products of the author's imagination or are used fictitiously. Any resemblance to actual persons, living or dead, events, or locales is entirely coincidental.

Acknowledgment

First, thanks must go out to the Higher Being for providing me with a sound body and mind; in addition to having the natural talent of writing and blessing me with the ability to tap into such an amazing part of life. Second, thanks most definitely go out to my Princess Ja'Calin. Third, Christina Deer and Pamela Valentine, thanks for being a huge help! Fourth, to my supporters and new readers for giving me a chance. Where in the world would I be without y'all?

Truth be told, I wouldn't have made it this far without anyone. I truly thank everyone for rocking with me. MUAH! Y'all make this writing journey enjoyable! I would like to thank everyone from the bottom of my heart for always rocking with the novelist kid from Alabama, no matter what I drop. Y'all have once again trusted me to provide y'all with quality entertainment.

Enjoy, my loves!

Chapter One

X

The hormones from being pregnant, on top of the feelings I was already holding in, were doing a severe number on my mental. I wasn't expecting for me to tell Bango how I really felt about his father coming after me. I didn't know how to perceive anything that I was going through or felt. However, I knew that I had to get away so that I could think properly. Ducked off in a corner to myself, once Bango and I separated for a shower, I tried giving myself a pep talk that didn't work at all. I was very relieved when Juvy called my phone to the point I had a smile on my face.

The brief conversation that Juvy and I had helped me to not focus so hard on my problems. On the contrary, we did come up with a plan to stop two common issues that we had— Reggio and the Jocktons. The plan was so good. Fuck that...it was the best! While I was on the phone, I hoped that he wasn't going to be anywhere close by when I walked out of the bathroom because what happened between the two of us earlier wasn't supposed to have happened. Our conversation was cut short because of Bango catching me coming out of the bathroom with only a towel wrapped around my body.

Pushing him away from my cotton covered body was not a success. I quickly ended the call once his long, light-skinned fingers traveled straight to my hot spot. There was no need in protesting against what was about to happen—my cat was yearning for some loving, and he was eager to give it to me. Not to mention, that we had a helluva chemistry.

On the stairwell, he gave me the business. I had never been fucked on the stairs, and when I say that I was like a toddler having a falling out spell—I did just that begging for him to get out of me. He wasn't overly rough to the point I was fighting him off me; he was passionately rough!

The type of intimacy that was going on between the two of us was that 'I'm sorry,' 'I miss you,' 'Bitch, I hate you,' 'Nigga, why you left me when I needed you the most?' type of sexing. My knees were wobbling and before we knew it, I was collapsing. Of course, he picked me up. Safely in his arms, he walked me to the master bedroom. Placing me gently on the soft, dark blue covers of his specially made circular bed, I was asleep as soon as my head hit the cold, firm pillow with Bango holding me close to him.

I didn't know how long I slept peacefully, or if I even slept peacefully. There was a real-life situation that took place when I was younger, in which I dreamt of often. Knowing that I may have fought in my sleep, because of that dream, my eyes landed on a red eyed, caring Bango.

"Did I hurt you?" I asked in a low tone as I continued to gaze into his hazel-green eyes.

"No," he replied, gently rubbing my face.

"Cool. I think it's time that I head home," I stated as I lifted my shoulders and head away from the pillow.

"Nawl, sit back, be quiet, and think. You are having that dream for a reason. You talked during the entire dream. You said the same shit you did the day that it happened. I won't bother you, but you need to pay close attention to that dream. It might can help us."

Intrigued by the word *us*, I kept my mouth shut and did as he instructed. Looking up at the ceiling, I went back to that day in August of 2008 when Bango and I escaped to The W in Atlanta, Georgia, followed by fleeing to Gulf Shores.

The recurrent dream that always brought on a fighting spell was the night I killed Tony's father, which led to whomever I was lying beside to wake me—that's where I knew I had to start at.

"X! X! Ma, it's just a dream. Wake up. You are in safe hands, please wake up," Bango stated in a soothing tone as he was holding on to me tightly, planting little kisses on my forehead.

"I'm... I'm... I'm oookaay," I stammered as I slowly opened my eyes.

"Look at me, X. Let me know it's real, mane. You got a nigga scared right now."

"I'm okay."

I kept saying I was okay, but I really wasn't. I was shook. That damn dream was going to get someone seriously hurt. I felt everything in that dream as if it was happening to me all over again. As Bango was caring for me, all I could do was lie to him like I was alright. I had to give myself a pep talk. It took me awhile to get my thoughts together. When I did, I was still slightly distraught. Looking around the hotel room, I realized that we were on the floor butt ass naked. Bango had a serious hold on me until I told him to ease up some.

"You gotta get your breathing under control. Follow me," he stated as he turned my head toward him. I couldn't look him in the face, so I averted my eyes elsewhere. He was doing breathing exercises, and as he commanded, I followed him.

"That's it. That's it," he stated with a small smile.

Shortly after, my breathing started to settle down. I was ashamed to look Bango in the face. I didn't want him to know that I had a weak spot. He might think he could run over me. I knew he was going to ask me about the episode because this was the second time that I've had one when with him. As I was secured in his arms, our cell phones started ringing, but neither of us paid any attention to them.

"I'm okay. I'm sorry if I put my hands on you in the wrong way," I stated in a childlike voice as I got up off the floor. I dashed to the bathroom because I didn't want him to see me like that anymore—distraught.

"How often do you have that dream?" he asked, standing in front of the bathroom door. I tried my best not to look at what was hanging between his legs, but hell, he had a nice size dick. My goodness! Just the right size, length, and girth...I see how I got... never mind.

"It seems like more now," I responded, as I looked at my appearance in the mirror. I resembled a person that was scared shitless with my eyes red and bucked.

"That was your first kill, huh?" he inquired, coming into the bathroom and sitting on the vanity. I couldn't produce any words. Therefore, I nodded my head.

"Yeah, those are the worst. You are okay. That's the most important part. But umm, how in the hell am I supposed to explain these scratches and shit on me," he laughed as he rubbed my right cheek gently. I turned on the cold water and splashed my face several times.

"You don't explain shit to anyone, remember?" I replied in a matter-of-fact tone, staring at my wet face in the mirror. With my peripheral vision, I saw Bango getting a small, white wash cloth. I held out my hand, but he ignored it.

"Yeah, you right," he chuckled softly, turning my head toward him and patting my face dry.

"Thank you," I voiced not looking him in the eyes.

"No problem, X, but umm, I've been thinking about something real heavy, and I might need your help with it."

"Damn, you already coming to me with a proposition, huh?" I inquired, as I tried not to observe his physique.

"I have to because if they pose a problem for me, they will certainly pose a problem for you later on down the road."

"I need a drink after that dream, and I will most definitely need a drink after I hear you out," I stated, grabbing his hand and leading him to the room's liquor bar.

"How in the fuck you got so thick? You wasn't built like this when I first met you?" he asked, as he rubbed my ass. I knew it wasn't going to be long before he started with the shenanigans. I was actually glad that he began his normal foolery, since it allowed me to get my mind off that damn dream.

"Thickness comes with time and taking care of your body."

"Or you got some nigga digging that ass out," he laughed.

"You too much for me," I laughed, fixing us something to drink. I motioned for us to sit on the bed so that we could talk.

"Tell me what's up?" I probed, sipping the nastiest liquor in the world, Jose Cuervo.

"I might need your help with killing Eric and J. The two guys that's on my cre—" he stated before I cut him off. He was crossing one hell of a line, trying to off his partners, and I didn't like that one bit.

"Why in the fuck would you want to do that?" I asked, getting up from the bed and moving quickly to the closet. I knew right then that he couldn't be trusted. I had the closet door opened with my hand on my tool when he spoke sternly.

"Girl, get yo' ass on this damn bed. Hear a nigga out," he demanded sternly, looking absolutely delicious.

I turned around on my right heel and stared at his sexy ass. With my facial expression stern, he didn't say shit until I allowed him to talk. While I narrowed in on him, trying to figure his ass out, I couldn't avoid observing his physique. That motherfucker was beautifully crafted. His amazing looks and demeanor had me all in—the nigga was a boss just like me, and I wasn't going to lie like it didn't turn me on.

The streets called him Bango, but Marcus Johnson was the name his mother gave him. He was half-Italian and half-black with jet black hair that was cut low with mad waves, black, bushy eyebrows, and hazel-green eyes. He was somewhere around six foot two and weighed about one-hundred and some odd pounds. That nigga had flawless skin, which he took pride in putting ink to his yellow skin. Just the right size lips, hands, feet, and dick... oh, I already said that earlier. Bango was nicely toned in all the right areas and had a beautiful smile set off with eight shining, gold teeth at the bottom and crisp, pearly whites where there wasn't gold. Even his veins were speaking volumes to me!

"Hmm, hmm. Damn you zoned out, didn't it? All eyes on this dick and shit," he voiced as he got up to do the beat it up dance. Shaking my head, I laughed.

"You are a pain in my ass… you do know that, right?" I laughed as he strolled and danced toward me.

Within a split second of me joking with Bango, we heard a loud thud by the handle of our room door. Once we heard that thud, we were instantly placed in survival mode. As the door was kicked opened, Bango was already on the floor beside the bed, and I hit the floor with my PX-4 in my hand, crouching on my stomach as I peeked around the short, tan sofa. All I thought about was us making it out of there alive. Therefore, I aimed my PX-4 at the door and let that bitch loose. I didn't stop pressing the trigger until I saw people crawling on the ground to get to safety. That's when I heard people screaming and shouting that someone was shooting. I looked at Bango and mouthed for him to stay put. I reached into the closet, grabbed an extra clip, and put it in my tonka toy. I hopped up quickly and ran toward the other side of the bed by the wall. I slowly peeked around the corner into the hallway. With my gun extended out, I ambled toward the door. When I got to the big hole where the door was moments ago, I saw two individuals in full tactical gear stretched across the floor, on their backs. The patrons of the hotel's third floor were running wild and on the phone with police talking about shooting that took place in The W.

"Let's motherfucking go!" I yelled as I ran back to the room and gathered all my things.

We were asshole naked trying to gather our shit and put on clothes, so the adrenaline rush that flooded me was phenomenal. It didn't take me but a hot second to put on a casual grey dress and slip on my gray Keds. I didn't have to tell Bango anything twice. He was on his feet putting on clothing and slanging his stuff in a Nike bag at the same time.

I had a special device that I liked to use only when things got sticky. Before I decided to press the button on that device, I pressed the panic button on another handy device Ruger gave me. I was ready to press the button on my favorite device, so I told Bango to run fast as he could toward the farthest exit, which was seventeen rooms away. Before he passed the sofa, I pressed the red button on that device and hauled ass.

By the time I passed the eighth room, my device went off. The screams grew louder, and my legs ran faster; I saw Bango looking back. I told him not to look back and to keep running. I didn't have to look back to know that paper, cotton, wood, and glass was everywhere. If a motherfucker was near that room, they were some dead asses! I had a wide smile on my face as I sped past Bango.

"Catch up, young buck," I stated as I ran straight toward the exit door, kicking that motherfucker open. I ran down the three flights of stairs. I felt my cell phone ringing, but there was no way in hell I was going to answer it. I was on a mission to get the fuck out of dodge.

When we made it outside, I ran past the people that were out there trying to figure out what was going on. I busted the driver's windows on my whip, unlocked the door, and plopped my ass in the seat. As I was hotwiring The Beast, Bango was looking in all directions. Five seconds of me touching the wires together, The Beast made the most beautiful noise.

"Get the fuck out the way, if you value your fucking life!" I yelled, as I backed up my 1976 Caprice. Once I put the gearshift in drive, I fled out of The W's parking lot, aiming for I-85 South—Alabama bound.

"What the fuck just popped off back there, mane? Are you okay?" Bango questioned as he was shaking his head.

"Yeah, I'm good. Are you? Will you please look in my bag, get my phone, and hold on to the two button?"

"I'm gucci, Ma. Yeah, I'll do that for you."

After he retrieved my phone, he did what I asked of him. He placed the phone on speaker. I don't even think the phone rung on Ruger's end.

"Yo, Chief. What the fuck going on? Where are you?" Ruger rattled off.

"Assassins," was all that I could say.

"Who's team?"

"Italians... the up north ones."

"Where are you?"

"Heading away from the scene. I need the cleanup crew at The W. I don't want a motherfucker to say shit."

"Where are you headed?" Ruger asked again but in an agitated tone.

"I'll let you know when I get there," I hurriedly said into the phone before hanging it up.

"Mane, whenever we touch down somewhere, I'm truly going to fuck the shit out of you. You did some boss ass shit back there. I'm truly in awe. Now, I know you are the perfect person to help me."

***

Every blue moon, I would link up with Bango in The A or whatever city he would like to visit. He was a pretty good friend of mine that I occasionally let get on me, or I on him—whoever had the balls to take matters into their hands. I really took a liking to him when he tried to offer me a gig on his team when he was first in the game. That was the funniest shit in the world. I had to know who he was and look out for him. He let it be known that he was the real deal—no balls, no talking, down to ride, a true soldier. Some in my crew said that I had a weak spot for Bango, and they were right. He was cool peeps that knew how to lay the dick and mouth down. I was just a female to him, not the most powerful gangster/dope manufacturer around. I could actually let my hair down around him, but at times, it was hard to do so.

"You want me to drive?" Bango asked, interrupting my thoughts.

"No, but we need to change cars."

"We can hide The Beast at my getaway house two miles from here. We'll hop in one of my rides that I have stashed there. Is that cool with you, ma?" he asked in that southern voice of his.

"Yes."

We were in Columbus, Georgia, the country part. Even though it was eight o'clock at night, I saw that it had a lot to offer me—solitude. I loved the country side of any area, the green grass and no neighbors. Ten minutes of enjoying the scenery, I was pulling onto a gravel road and fled down it. In front of me was the most beautiful single family bricked home. The front yard was massive, but it was not decorated at all.

"Pull around back," Bango stated casually.

"Okay, but umm...why in the hell you don't have this place set up with some type of décor?" I asked, as I pulled around back.

Laughing, he responded, "Because I'm a man. We don't give a damn about decorating outside. That's a female thing."

"Tuh, I beg to differ, friend," I snickered lightly as I thought about the beautifully decorated homes of my ex-lover, Francesco.

"I want you to pull up to that shed. Once I back out my Escalade, I want you to pull in." I nodded my head and once he had his truck out of the shed, I did as he instructed. I cut the engine off, grabbed our bags, and exited my noise maker.

"Let's hit the road. We never decided on a place, X. Where are we going?" he asked while taking the bags from me.

"I have a condo in Gulf Shores. Let's head there."

"Damn, I get to fuck you on the beach?" he joked. I looked at him with a stern face, but I quickly changed it once he started doing the beat it up dance.

"Is that your trademark dance, guy?"

"When I'm around you."

"Get your ass in the truck, sir," I commanded nicely.

"Damn, you sound like that X I conduct business with. When we get down there to this condo, can you be that hard-ass X? I'm tired of that submissive, X," he replied with a sneaky smile on his face.

"Let's be serious now. I gotta figure out what in the fuck just happened at The W. Wait a damn minute, why are you still with me after what just happened?"

"Nih, guh, you know damn well we have been in way more shit than that. Remember Moscow?" he laughed. That reminder caused me to blush and bust out laughing. I hopped in the passenger seat and buckled up without saying anything else about Moscow.

As we left the getaway house, Bango and I didn't talk much. I wasn't really in the conversing mood, since I was trying to figure out what in the fuck was really going on. Four hours later, we were pulling up at my lovely condo in Orange Beach. We grabbed our luggage and headed to the quiet but comforting four-bedroom and two bath living quarters. Upon entering, a smile spread across my face once I smelled the Hawaiian Glade air freshener, felt the cool air, and the aura of peace that the condo provided. I walked toward my room and plopped down on the bed with my duffle bag still on my back. Bango wasn't too far behind me.

"I'm assuming this is your personal space," he voiced quietly as he looked around the room.

"Indeed it is," I replied, smiling brightly.

"You have weird but exquisite taste," he confessed as he touched several of my handmade craft pieces from Africa.

"Why thank you, sir."

I pulled off my shoes and slid them under the bed. I didn't want to talk about the shooting that took place at The W, but I had too. I knew that Francesco was going to be the next person that I talked to once I was finished chopping it up with Ruger and Bango. Who were the Italians really after, me or Bango? Why would they be after either of us, especially me? I thought as I glanced at Bango.

"Bango?"

"What's up, Ma?" he replied as he took off his shirt and started flexing his chest muscles. I ignored him and went straight into business mode.

"Have you done anything to piss anyone off... such as the Italians? I sure as hell know I didn't."

I gave him my undivided attention because I was always able to read him when he was lying, and now was not the time to lie.

"No. I don't fuck with the Italians at all...well...except for my dad, and he keeps me a secret, so no."

"Do you think someone could've found out about you?"

"No."

"Okay. Well, I gotta call my eyes and ears and see what the fuck is really going on."

"Bet. I'm finna hit the shower then I'm coming to lay underneath you... that's cool?"

"Oh, you asking me now?" I laughed. With a smile on his face, he walked out of my room and into the bathroom.

I pulled my phone out of my bra and held down on the number two button. On the fourth ring, Ruger answered his phone, "Chief? You good?"

"Yes. I'm at the chilly on the hilly."

Chilly on the hilly was the code name for my condo in Orange Beach.

"Roger that. You be safe. Everything is washed and folded."

"Great. Have a nice night. I'll let you know how the vacay went once I touch back in town."

"Okay, and you have a nice night as well. Oh, don't come back pregnant," he demanded roughly.

"Bye, Ruger," I stated sternly before hanging the phone up in his face.

My second task was to contact Francesco. He had eyes and ears everywhere, which was great for me. It took him a few seconds to answer the phone, but he did nonetheless.

"My beautiful, semi-chocolate Queen, how are you?" Francesco questioned in that strong, Italian accent of his.

"I'm fine... I guess. Hey, baby, I need your eyes and ears now more than ever. Two Italians tried to hit me tonight. Can you figure out why and exactly who they were?"

"When and where?"

"In Atlanta at The W."

"How do you know they were Italian?"

"Because the two damn idiots that they sent had 'morte prima di disonore' around their necks," I informed him as I rolled my neck from side-to-side.

Morte prima di disonore in English meant death before dishonor. Most of the people in the Italian Mafia didn't have tattoos visible, but those two idiots did, which made things easy for me.

"Oh, wow! They are most definitely with the mafia up north. Give me a few days to get you the information you are seeking. In the meantime, be careful, my beautiful Queen."

After I ended the call, I remembered that my cell phone was vibrating back in Atlanta, and I never checked it out. The top of the display screen showed an envelope, and I slid it down. I had four text messages from Tyke. Shit! I thought as I opened them up, with shaky hands.

While reading his texts, I felt like a hopeless child. He was cursing me out for what happened in The A. I wondered how he knew what took place. Wanting to ask him, I quickly changed my mind upon seeing a soaking wet Bango.

"What got you in deep thought?" he asked, licking his lips.

"Nothing," I lied, trying not to look at those inches.

"A lie ain't shit for a Queenpin to tell."

"Bango, don't come for me unless you want to be came'd on," I replied seductively before I licked my lips.

"And exactly how many times have you done that since we linked up and will continue to do this entire weekend?" he laughed after walking toward me, pushing my legs open and diving his head in between my legs.

"Bango, are you familiar with the saying 'morte prima di disonore?'" I asked him soon as I was finished thinking.

"Yeah, why?" he replied as he rested his head in the palm of his right hand.

"The two guys that were sent to that room had that saying around their necks."

"Then that means they were a part of my father's organization. Most of those guys have it on the lower portion of their backs. Do you think that my father sent them at you?"

"Without a doubt. Your father was behind the hit. He wants me dead for some reason, and it has nothing to do with me shooting you or getting into a shootout with you. This shit is deeper than that."

"We need to set a trap for my father and his men. This shit must be put to an end, once and for all. This shit sounds like it has Tyke written all over it," Bango stated through clenched teeth.

I wanted to tell him about Juvy and my plans of putting his father to an end, but I decided against it. The less Bango knew the better. I didn't want him in harm's way again because of his funky ass father.

Chapter Two

Taea

Wednesday, December 20, 2017

Bango had me so fucked up in the head to the point I jumped back on a plane with my babies and headed back to Alabama. He thought he was going to reminisce about a bitch and have the temptation of bedding the hoe while I was in another state but that wasn't going to happen. Oh no, he had me completely fucked up if that's what he thought. I didn't tell anyone that we were coming back. I paid extra money for the Christmas gifts to be shipped to my grandmother's house. By the time the gifts arrived, the twins and I would be comfortably sitting at her table.

Touching down in Birmingham at approximately one-thirty in the afternoon, I rented a car and fled the city, aiming for my hometown. Since my babies and I were on our way back to Alabama, not one time today have I talked to my husband. When I talked to him last night, he sounded preoccupied, and I tried to think positive about things. However, his old ways got the best of me. I knew people wondered why in the hell I married him, knowing that he had whorish ways, and honestly, I began to ponder the same thing. After the first shootout with X, that left him paralyzed for a short amount of time, Bango was in bad shape mentally and physically.

Every day, he vowed that he was done with hoe hopping and dealing drugs. After he realized that the streets truly didn't love anybody, he left it behind. I could honestly say that I saw improvement in him as my man and person. So, it was nothing for me not to think twice about marrying him. I'm not going to lie that I should've thought twice about marrying his ass, especially with him telling me that he wanted to fuck a bitch that should be dead.

With the twins sleeping peacefully in their car seats, the hour and some odd minutes ride to Montgomery went by in a blur. I was pulling into the double-sided neighborhood of Braisedlawn with a pounding heart and clammy hands.

One side of the community was the rowdy side, and the other side wasn't. I was glad that my grandmother and Grandma Toot lived on the quiet side. As I topped their street, I squinted my eyes toward Grandma Toot house to see if Bango's car was either parked in the yard or on the street.

"Where this bitch at?" I stated angrily as I crept closer to the grandmothers' homes and noticed that Snoogi's Suburban wasn't anywhere in the vicinity.

Snatching my phone from the console of the Hyundai Accent, I unlocked my screen and held down the number three while making a left turn into my grandmother's beautifully decorated yard.

On the third ring, my husband's strong, sexy voice answered the phone out of breath, "Hello."

"What you doing?" I asked nonchalantly.

"Running."

"Um hmm," I replied curtly as I tried to remain calm because he could actually be out running.

"What are you and the twins doing?" he asked as I listened carefully for anything that was out of the ordinary in the background.

"Cooling. They are sleeping," I said as I saw my grandmother walk out of the front door toward the car with her right hand over the top of her eyebrows.

As she turned around on her heels and waltzed back toward the front door of her home, I wanted to chuckle at her extra behind given that the sun wasn't even shining that brightly.

However, the wind was blowing, and that brought a quizzical look upon my face. Therefore, I zoned in on Bango's end to see if he was indeed out running.

"Give them a kiss for me."

No wind blowing in the background, but I'm looking at the leaves on the trees blowing hard, I thought as I noticed my grandmother looking toward the car.

Once I waved at her, I held up one finger, signaling that I would be out in a minute. What really set me the fuck off was that I didn't hear any wind rippling in the background, and I heard a door close in the background.

"Umm, you say you are running and such, but I don't hear any wind blowing in the background. However, I did just hear a door close. So, I'mma need for you to tell me what the fuck you are doing," I stated with an attitude.

Silence.

"I know your motherfucking ass heard me!" I shouted in the car, quickly forgetting my sleeping babies were in the backseat.

"Damn, Taea, has it ever occurred to you that a nigga might be at the gym?" he asked casually before laughing. Not seeing shit funny, I brought something to his attention.

"If you were at the gym, like you say, then why I don't hear other people talking or at least hear the workout machines going?"

"As usual, Snoogi paid for the place to be shut down for an hour. He's still skeptical about the entire X thing, so he's being extra cautious," Bango stated in a matter-of-fact tone.

It was mighty cute how he had to throw Snoogi's name up in the mix, so that I couldn't argue with him.

Giving what Bango said was plausible, I hit him with, "Is Snoogi there with you?"

"Yep," Bango spat eagerly into the phone.

"Okay," I sighed in relief.

At that particular moment, I was about to open my mouth to apologize for suggesting that Bango was up to no good, but my motherfucking ass saw Snoogi's truck sliding down the road; while his pale behind was hanging out the window and smiling at some young girls that were standing in front of a black jeep, three houses up from the grandmothers' houses.

Shaking with anger, I spat, "Bitch, you lie too much for me. I see Snoogi on our grandmothers' street. There's no need for me to even press the issue with you. Just know that once the holiday season is over with... your ass will be on the way back to being a single man."

Sighing heavily before responding, I knew that Bango was choosing his words carefully.

"Taea, you in New York. How you gon' tell me where Snoogi at?" he inquired nonchalantly.

As he was trying to be a smarty about the situation instead of coming clean, I politely took a picture of Snoogi hopping out of his car and quickly sent it to my lying ass husband.

Within seconds he replied, "Taea, I didn't mean to lie to you. I just don't want you worrying about me... that's all. No, I'm not at the gym. I'm actually getting ready to head out to analyze some shit."

"Yeah, I bet," I huffed angrily into the phone.

The line went quiet on his end, and I pressed my ear closer into the phone so that I could understand what was going on. My intuition told me something wasn't right, but I couldn't quite put my finger on it. Come hell or high water, Snoogi was going to tell me where in the fuck my husband was. So, that I could deliver him the best ass whooping and to inform him face to face that either he was getting his ass on a plane or we were over with!

Hanging up the phone and throwing it on the seat, I opened the door and hollered, "Snoogi! Come here." Turning around to see who was calling his name, I made sure to wave my hand so that he saw me. As he began to hop in his truck, he pulled his cell phone out of his front pocket, put it to his ear, and hopped in the driver's seat.

"I bet that bastard, Bango, is calling him," I said to myself as I watched Snoogi slowly drive away from the young broads he was rapping with.

As I had my eyes locked in on Snoogi's truck, I saw him roll down his window. Coming to a complete stop inches away from my grandmother's home, he hollered, "Taea, that was an important call. I gotta go."

Wickedly laughing, I nodded my head and slid back in the front seat. Starting the engine on the car, I was ready to follow his ass because I knew without a doubt that he was going where my husband was. As Snoogi peeled away from Grandma Toot's house, I placed the gearshift in reverse and started to back out until my grandmother flagged me down.

"Uggh, what do she want? I need to be behind Snoogi before I lose him," I stated aloud as I rolled down the passenger window at the same time my phone began to ring.

"Where are you going?" she asked loudly as I ignored the ringing phone.

"To find something out. I'll be back," I told her as I eased my foot off the brake.

"Get them babies in this house. Nothing is more important than their well-being. Whatever you are seeking can wait. If it's meant for you to know, then it will surely come to light," she told me in that 'don't argue with me' tone.

Feeling myself about to break down and pitch a full fit, I placed the gearshift in drive and pulled back into her yard. When I unlocked the doors, Grandma Sue grabbed MarTaea's car seat and diaper bag at the same time I opened the driver's door. Stepping out into the slightly breezy air, I quickly closed the driver's door and opened the back door so that I could grab my son's car seat and diaper bag. Throwing the blanket over his face, I had a mean facial expression across mine. I tried not to think about my grandmother's statement of things coming to the light, but I couldn't help myself. The 'what if's' started getting to me.

Along the way to my grandmother's front door, tears were sliding down my face and I announced, "I think I'm going to divorce Bango, Grandma."

***

"I don't give a fuck what you got going on, Marcus?" I heard my grandmother say as I wiped the crust out of my eyes.

From the soft snoring coming from in front of me, I knew the twins were still sleeping. With a pleasant smile upon my face as I gazed at my babies, I sighed heavily. It was time to mentally prepared myself for the conversation I was going to have with my husband.

Eager to see Bango's handsome face as my grandmother chewed him out, I quickly but carefully hopped out of the bed. Slipping my feet into my soft, comfortable pink house shoes, I slid through the half-opened, ivory hued bedroom door and waltzed into the newly decorated, African American woman chef themed cooking quarters. I swore my grandmother changed the décor in her home more than she bought panties and bras.

Peeping my head into the kitchen, I saw Bango standing in a black Ralph Lauren collared shirt, denim jeans, and black boots. On his head was a black Saints snapback hat which was cocked to the right. A gold pair of diamond stud earrings was tucked into his earlobes. As I loved the sight of my husband, I also hated the sight of him. Seeing him, reminded me of how much he takes me for granted and how dumb I am for him.

"Hey, baby," he announced sexily to me as he broke the stares between him and my grandmother.

"Hi. Where have you been?" I probed, walking further into the kitchen.

"Taking care of business," he replied quickly and then continued, "Daddy's babies must be sleep."

"Yep," I responded curtly with squinty eyes.

"Marcus, you and I ain't done talking," my grandmother stated in a matter-of-fact tone.

"Yes, ma'am," he said as he placed his eyes back on Grandma Sue, who was standing in a stance that let Bango know that she wasn't playing with him.

Grandma Sue was the sweetest person I knew besides Grandma Toot, but when she's rubbed the wrong way, she'll let you know and not in a pleasant manner either. My grandmother stood five feet seven, around one hundred and sixty pounds, brown skin tone, and had a set of hands that would knock your ass out.

Susie Mae Gresham was well-educated, loving, and caring; on the other hand, she would tell you some things that would have your soul hurting. She'd been married once and vowed that she would never marry again. My grandfather was Benson Gresham. That man did the most while being married to her. He fucked her cousin, so now I saw why she didn't want to be bothered with the 'I do' skit. She was currently dating some dude that she'd been seeing off and on for two years. I truly thought if George Ferguson asked her to marry him, she would.

As I was thinking, Grandma Sue politely but rudely said, "You act like you don't have a whole fucking family that loves and cares about your yellow ass. You think my granddaughter won't leave you? Well, that ass better think again. I'm not going to let you destroy her and those precious babies. Whatever you got going on needs to cease now!"

With a smirk on my face, I sounded off with, "Hmm, hmm."

There was no need in me telling Grandma Sue to not go in, because he needed to hear someone other than me to tell him to get his shit together.

After I was done putting my three cents in, my grandmother turned her head toward me, smacked her lips while putting her hands on her thick hips, and said, "Shut yo' punk ass up. It's time for you to woman up now. I thought you would've learned a thing or two from that trifling ass Try-anything hoe! Get you a got-damn backbone, Taea."

  When my grandmother was done speaking, she marched away from the kitchen into the dining room, turned on her favorite Christmas music, and left Bango and me alone.

  The mentioning of that bitch Trylesha Devoner, aka Try, made my blood boil, and I stared at my husband nastily. Try was my ex–best friend that Bango was fucking around with behind my back. He supposedly had gotten her pregnant. She was indeed pregnant, but I whooped that baby out of that hoe's body for stepping to me one too many times, trying to explain her and Bango's situation. She learned real quick that I was nothing to toy with. She eventually stopped trying to reach out to me to explain her side of the story.

   With nothing to say to me, I took the initiative to probe more into my husband's thoughts and behavior.

"Do you still have those thoughts about that girl?" I questioned as I glared into his hazel-green eyes.

Exhaling heavily, he shook his head. I knew that he was a bold-faced lie. Therefore, I asked him again.

"Do you still have those thoughts, Bango?"

"Mane, I told you no. Change the subject, Taea."

"Is she dead?"

"Nope."

"You have until tomorrow to make the bitch have a death certificate," I voiced sternly, not taking my eyes off him.

"Look, your place is being my wife and the mother to our children. You ain't and never have been a street chick. Stay in a comfortable, safe place. Let me handle this," he commanded as we heard my grandmother sing along to "Silent Night" by The Temptations.

Before I spoke, I made sure that she wasn't in earshot of what I had to say. Upon me seeing that she wasn't, I let my husband have it.

"You act like you want to be single. Is that it, Bango? Do you want your free roaming ass life back? Because I surely can arrange that for you. I'm done putting up with the past. Dead the shit or lose your wife and children. We are on a different level than before you asked me to marry you. I'm not going for this shit! Do you understand me?"

"Taea, you ain't gotta do all that. I'm not going anywhere. So, chill and let's have a great holiday with our family and friends."

Looking at him like he lost his mind at the mentioning of friends, I had to remind him that I didn't have any since he wanted to fuck them all. Call me petty or whatever, I didn't give a damn. With a quizzical look upon his face, he opened his mouth to say something, but he knew to keep it shut. As he stared at me, he licked his thick, juicy lips and rubbed his hands together with a mischievous grin spread across his face.

"Nope...before you even ask me," I huffed, propping my right leg up. I depended on my toes to keep me stable.

Laughing, he responded, "You don't even know what I'm thinking."

"Shittin' me. I've known you all of my life."

"Come on, woman, and let's go spend some quality time with our kids," he voiced casually as he strolled closer to me, grabbed my hand, and pulled me close to him.

"I hate that I love you," I announced softly after I placed my head onto his chest.

"Shut up with that noise. I'm all yours."

For some strange reason, I didn't believe that, especially with X still living; on top of me knowing that they had history together. Once she was out of the picture, then I would know without a doubt that he was all mine.

Chapter Three

Juvy

Saturday, December 23rd

 Today was one sickening day for me. As I sat on Flema's porch, I shed tears and laughed. I reminisced on the first time I met her and how the feeling of being a lonely kid in downtown Miami flooded through my body. While I sat on her lonely brown and white porch, I felt like that same knotted-head kid who was dropped off in a country that I knew nothing about.

 All over again, I was lost and lonely. Not to mention, my heart was heavy from her actions. Flema was the one that told me that everything would be okay, and one day, I would find those responsible for killing my family and stripping my happy childhood away.

 It was thirty minutes past ten, and I was still all over the place. I didn't know whether to be pissed off at myself or at Flema for her no longer breathing. My heart and soul hurt due to the fact that I did her wrong when all she wanted was love from me. She fucked and sucked the Orgon brothers just to help me find some peace. True enough, that was some hoe shit, but she did that out of love for me. I felt responsible for her taking her life. I would've never thought she would do some shit like that.

Ding. Ding. Ding.

Taking a brief look at my phone, X's name popped up on the screen. With a faint smile upon my face, I unlatched my phone from the holster before sliding my finger across the answer option. As I said hello, I placed the phone to my right ear.

"Hey. How are you feeling?" her smooth, sweet voice inquired.

"Like shit. I feel responsible for all of this, X. Never would I have thought that she would kill herself," I voiced softly into the phone as I looked around Flema's neighborhood before placing my eyes on the beautiful blue, cloudless sky.

"You can't fault yourself, Juvian. She had her own mind, and she chose to end her life."

I loved how she called me Juvian, and truth be told, I never wanted her to stop saying it. I honestly preferred for her to call me Juvian versus Juvy.

"But, X, she was pregnant with my kid."

The line was silent for a while, causing me to check if she was still there.

"Hello?" I called out.

"I'm here. I'm just shocked by you saying that. It's rare that a woman would kill herself while being pregnant, or so I think."

Not knowing how to respond to her comment, all I could say was "hmm."

Tired of thinking with teary eyes, I asked, "How are you? What's going on up there? Are you in a secured place until I leave from down here?"

Sighing heavily, she responded, "I'm okay... I think. I believe I fucked up, Juvy."

Alarm rising in me instantly, which showed in my tone when I asked, "How?"

"Remember the night you called me and I told you I would talk to you later?"

"Nawl, I remember the phone hanging up," I laughed, which caused her to softly chuckle, followed by her telling me to shut up.

"Anyways, smarty. I slept with the dude that I supposedly killed on his wedding day."

Completely blown by what she confessed, I replied, "Explain."

As X told me how things popped off and ended during her and Bango's most recent encounter, I found myself jealous and somewhat pissed off at her. I know I didn't have a reason to be that way toward her, but that's how I felt. I couldn't let her know how I felt about that since we weren't going steady. Twiddling my fingers to keep from telling her a thing or two, I closed my eyes and thought about how she looked in my arms when we were together. Briefly zoning completely out, X brought me back into reality with her bossy, professional tone.

"Juvian King!" she sounded off.

"Shit! Yes, ma'am?" I replied, in a scared soldier's voice-- who was in basic training for the armed forces.

"You so damn goofy. Did you hear me?"

"No. I was thinking about the way you looked as you laid in my arms."

Silence.

"Did you hear me, X?"

"Yes," she stated in a child-like tone.

"I love being in your presence and talking to you. So from time to time, I drift off with thoughts of you," I confessed, standing up and fixing my fitted black suit and ensuring that my shiny, black gators didn't have a speck of dirt on them.

"Your emotions are all over the place. Flema's situation is clouding your thinking process. Get to the funeral, and I'll call you once I think you are alone. Okay?"

Not wanting to get off the phone with her, I tried to bring up anything just to keep hearing her voice while fumbling with the lone necklace around my neck. Nothing I said worked on that woman!

"I'll call you once I think the funeral and burial is over with, Juvian King. Now, go and say your final goodbyes."

Click.

Looking at my screen, I had to see if that heifer really hung up on me. Shaking my head, it was a known fact that bossy chick hung it up without a moment's hesitation. Hopping into my ride, I prayed for Flema's soul and tried asking God to forgive me for how I acted toward her. After I was done praying for myself and Flema, I made sure to say a long, special prayer for the one female that I grew to like on a personal level.

***

Friendship Missionary Baptist Church was packed to capacity. Half of the people there didn't even like Flema because of me. Shaking my head at the fuckery that people did, I slowly strolled toward her casket with my eyes glued on her coral resting place. Clenching my badly burned hands, I felt anger rising in me as I saw Rondon stand tall and mean mug me.

What in the fuck is this nigga doing down here? I thought as I nodded my head and gave that fuck nigga a fake smile.

As I kept it moving, I saw Wilema grab his wrist and shake her head.

That nigga don't want none of me, and that's on gawd. Why in the fuck is he down here in the first place? I thought as I moved closer to Flema's casket.

My somewhat of a first love hardened face was the reason I stopped wondering why X's goon was at the funeral. The longer I stared at her face, the louder her mother cried out, and the more fucked up I felt inside. The beautiful ivory dress with floral embellishments rested perfectly against her cold, lifeless body. Lightly hued makeup complimented her final attire. Soft curls formed a halo around her head.

Bending down to kiss Flema on her forehead, her mother yelled out, "Get away from her. You are the reason she's dead, Juvy!"

"Calm down, momma," Wilema said sadly.

Turning around to stare Wilema and her family in the face, I chuckled and shook my head. Not the one to cause a scene during such an inappropriate time, I politely walked over to Flema's family and gave them my condolences. That damn mother of Flema and Wilema's spat on my shoes, and it took everything in me not to choke her ass out. Instead, I replied, "Sorry for your loss."

Walking off, Rondon mumbled something. Quickly turning around, I voiced loudly, "Don't mumble, little nigga. Speak your damn mind!"

"You heard me, fuck nigga. You are a low life ass bitch boy," he piped, strolling toward me with his chest poked out.

"Not here, y'all! This is my sister's homegoing celebration," Wilema yelled as Rondon took off running toward me.

Ready to set some shit off, I stood still. Soon as he was in arm's reach, I slammed my fist into his face. Immediately, blood spilled from his mouth and nose. When he stumbled back into two guys that were trying to get out of the way, I was on his ass, giving him a royal ass whooping. As people in the front pews moved out of the way, Wilema and others were screaming for us to stop.

In the middle of the church I heard, "That's why I hate coming down here with these ghetto ass folks. Jetson, go and get your damn son. He's been acting differently ever since he got some ass from that little bitch, X'Zeryka!"

At the mention of X's first name, I drilled my fists into Rondon's face. Feeling hatred toward him, I let him know that I didn't like him or the fact that he was fucking X.

Laughing at the same time three big niggas snatched me off him, Rondon had the nerve to say, "That's why she's mine and not yours. I got her pregnant, not you. Nigga, X, is all mine!"

Doubly heated at him for mentioning that he got her pregnant, I spat angrily, "Who said the baby is yours, lil' nigga? Keep in mind, I made love to her on several occasions. Remember when Ruger had to stitch up my knee? Well, fuck boy, I had just got done blessing her with these inches!"

Shrugging the guys off me, I held a mean gaze as I slowly backed away from the scene. Wilema had a jealous look upon her face, and I didn't give two fucks. I was ready for her to say something, so I could burst her damn bubble.

"Once again, Juvy, you have found a way to fuck up things for my daughter," Wilema's mother spat as she wiped underneath her eyes.

"Lady, fuck you! You wasn't saying shit when I was paying all of your bills, once George left your ass for that white woman he sitting by. You surely wasn't saying shit, once I moved y'all out of the projects into that nice four bedroom home you reside in now! You ain't gotta worry about seeing my face anymore. She's dead now! So, good fucking bye!" I shouted while staring her down.

The entire church gasped after I was done speaking. Walking away from the madness, all eyes were on me. Folks in the back of the church were whispering; while those in the front talked loudly about what happened moments ago.

Before I made it to the church doors, Rondon shouted, "I'mma see you soon, nigga!"

Coming to a complete halt with my hands together and facing the door, I replied sternly and confidently, "I'll be waiting on you while I'm laid up with X, bitch nigga!"

Chapter Four

Rondon

The learning of Flema's passing didn't bother me much since she and I really weren't that close. True enough, we talked from time to time, but I mostly conversed with her when I wanted to know something or when she was seeking my help in finding out information. Flema's mother was my father's third cousin, which made Flema my fourth cousin.

My father rarely brought us down to Miami to learn about our roots or for us to meet our family members. He barely talked about his parents and grandparents. Why? I couldn't answer that question, nor did I really care. With my parents, I learned quickly not to ask them shit, especially my mother. If they wanted us to know something, they would tell us.

After the incident between Juvy and me, my brothers and father made me go outside. Oh, my mother never shut her damn mouth from the time she told my father to come and get me for acting an ass. All I saw was red from the time Juvy strolled out of the church until I scanned the parking lot seeking his ass out. I prayed that my eyes landed on him because there was going to be a round two, and he was going to die.

With no luck in finding him or his Hummer, my mother was the primary target as she exploded about my behavior and X. I tolerated her mouth as long as I could by focusing on which route I was going to take back to Alabama. I was ready to check on my pregnant woman and make things right with her. X still hadn't reached out to me, and I was heavily pissed about that.

"I told you that whore of a woman isn't any good for you, Reginald. Look how you showed your ass at your cousin's funeral. For what, Reginald?" my mother spat as she scolded me.

"Momma, please be quiet. I'm tired of hearing your privileged voice," I responded sternly as I looked into her dark brown, oval-shaped face while enjoying the crisp, cool breeze.

She began talking shit, and I ignored her while entertaining the guests coming out of Friendship Missionary Baptist Church. The noise that mother of mine was making was for the birds. Her opinions and threats didn't mean a damn thing to me. My brothers and father tried to tell her to calm down, but she wasn't hearing it. Exhaling and inhaling deeply several times while thinking about X, I pulled out my phone and held down on the number two.

Upon the ringing of the phone, my mother's squeaky voice yelled, "That's it, Reginald. I'm cutting your ass off. You want to be down south showing your natural ass... you'll be showing it by being one broke ass nigga!"

"Momma, I don't need your fucking money. I got my own. That little change you send me ain't nothing compared to what I make monthly," I announced angrily at the same time I heard X's answering machine.

"Watch your mouth, boy," my father spoke sternly as he adjusted his black three-piece suit.

"Mane, whatever. You sit back and let momma say and do whatever to us and you. Grow some balls, Dad," I huffed while shoving my phone into my front, right pocket.

"That's enough of the disrespect, Reginald," my oldest brother, Ronald, stated calmly as he strolled toward me with a blank facial expression.

"Ronald, you should be the main one disrespectful, especially since momma forced you to marry Jessica and had Trina shipped to another side of the world."

I wasn't seeking any confrontation with my brother, but he was after me for my comment. As soon as my statement left his mouth, Ronald didn't waste any time bum rushing me against the front of my car. Completely thrown off guard by his actions, it didn't take me long to jack his ass up.

"Shut your damn mouth, little brother," he hissed as I held on tightly to the collar of his shirt.

Ronald was six feet even, fair-skinned like our father with bushy, black eyebrows, brown eyes, and an athletic build. Ronald Jetson Martin was the perfect son in my parents eyes; he did what they told him to do without even questioning them, which made me sick to my stomach.

"Y'all cut it out," Roger, my second oldest brother, voiced as he came to break up the misunderstanding between Ronald and me.

Releasing Ronald, I began to laugh hysterically. Looking at my family, I dug in my back pocket and grabbed my keys. As I stared into their embarrassed faces, I hit the unlock button on my key fob. I was beyond pissed at today's events, starting from the moment I placed my eyes on that fuck nigga, Juvy!

Turning my back and strolling toward the driver's door, my mother spoke nastily to my father about my behavior, which provoked an argument amongst them. Meanwhile, I thought seriously about running their asses over and going on about my business. Climbing into my CL 500, I smelled the wonderful half smoked blunt. Comfortably placing my body in the driver's seat, I opened the ashtray, pulled the half of a blunt out, and fired it up. Inhaling, I closed the door on my car and started the engine.

Wanting to fuck with my family, I revved the engine several times before placing the gearshift in drive. The looks on their faces as I burnt rubber were priceless. They wanted an asshole, so I sat in my car, getting high, and giving them just what they wanted.

Once I was done with the little blunt, I rolled down my window, tossed it out, and sped away from Friendship Missionary Baptist Church's parking lot. I wanted some act right out of them, especially my mother. She had to learn to stay in her place. I was a grown man, and I didn't need for her to tell me what to do, when to do it, and how to go about doing it.

Regina Martin was one bossy woman. She had been that way since I came into the world. I didn't think she knew how to be a calm, cool, and collected person. Everything must go her way, or it was the highway for you. My father's passive ass just put up with her shit. I didn't see how in the hell he did it for thirty plus years. My brothers were a sucker for her. If she told them to snort powder, those fools would ask how many lines. That's how influential and powerful she was to them.

Out of my two brothers, Ronald was the one I felt bad for the most. Mother dictated everything and anything he did. Ronald and Trina Motley had been secretly dating since they were in junior high school all the way through high school. The reason they were secretly dating was because Trina didn't come from *our* side of the tracks. Meaning, she didn't live in a wealthy neighborhood and she didn't attend private schools. Ronald knew without a doubt that no matter how smart and well-behaved Trina was, our mother wasn't going for the *hood* girlfriend shit.

When Ronald turned eighteen, our mother found out about Trina and scolded him for four hours on how to properly get the *right* girlfriend and not some money hungry whore. Momma demanded that Ronald end the relationship with Trina. My brother was head over heels in love with Trina, so there was no way he would break up with her. Therefore, he continued to sneak around with her until the day that she disappeared.

That was the first time I had ever seen Ronald cry. My poor big brother cried for two months behind Trina's disappearance. He never knew what happened to her until he saw her parents one day, and they finally told him that our mother paid Trina's tuition and board to one of the finest universities in London, England. Right then, my twelve-year-old mind knew that our mother wasn't to be trusted. Of course, Ronald questioned our mother about it, and she was very nonchalant with her answer. The bitch was downright cold-hearted about the situation.

You see, our mother wanted Ronald to marry and build a family with someone with the same background as us. The broad he was married to was from a wealthy family, and she had a lighter skin tone than my parents, siblings, and myself. She was white! My mother owed Jessica Forlorn's father a favor. What the favor was that my mother owed the man, no one knows because she's hella bent on keeping her business hers.

Ring. Ring. Ring.

Looking down at my phone, I saw my mother's name displaying across the screen. Quickly pressing the ignore button, I hopped on the interstate, heading back to 'Bama. I had enough of Miami and the people that were closely related to me there. I had to get my girl back and make things right between the two of us. There was no way in hell that I was going to let another nigga destroy the bed that I made with X!

***

It was Christmas, and a nigga wasn't in the mood to celebrate a holiday. Therefore, the right person for me to pull up on was Ruger since he wasn't with the holiday shits no ways. As I pulled into Ruger's trailer lot around 2:00 a.m., I wondered for the one-hundredth time within the past two months why he didn't get him a house built.

For the life of me, I couldn't figure out why he chose to live in a manufactured home versus a house— not that I saw anything wrong with living in a trailer and not that anything was wrong with the nicely built crib of his. I would've expected for him to have at least two acres of land with a simple home planted on it.

Outside of The Savage Clique, Ruger was one weird individual. He never went on dates, never brought a female to a social event, and never talked about or visited his family. The only reason we knew when his birthday was because X always made him a cake on June 10th. What I knew of Ruger was very little. I knew that he was a destructive asshole, he loved fast food, smoked Kool cigarettes, and didn't like rap music. He was one quiet individual outside of the jokes he provided every now and again.

Hopping out of my car, I ambled toward the white and tan, three-bedroom and one and half bath living quarters of my partner. His yard was as simple as the decor inside. No flowers or lounging chairs were on the front or back porches.

"What are you doing here?" Ruger spoke coolly from the left of me.

Straining my eyes to see him, I replied, "Nigga, exactly where are yo' black ass at?"

"Posted behind the second tree. I saw one of Reggio's Suburban trucks cruising through these streets about six hours ago. I'm on high alert mode. Have you talked to X?" he responded, walking closer to me. The only way I knew that he was strolling toward me was because I heard him stepping on a twig.

"The last time I talked to her was some days ago in Auburn. She still isn't answering the phone for me. Have you talked to her?" I voiced as he planted his body inches away from mine.

"She won't respond to any of my texts or calls. Wait... did you say that you saw her in Auburn?" he inquired, firing up a cigarette.

"Yep. She was talking to some dude...a baby D-boy compared to us."

"A big, dark-skinned dude?" he asked before inhaling his nicotine stick.

"Yeah."

Immediately, I wanted to know who the cat was since Ruger already knew who I was talking about.

"What in the fuck is she doing talking to that nigga?" he piped nastily.

"Your guess is just as good as mine," I voiced quickly and then continued, "Who is the nigga?"

"Juan Forrester. A dude she keeps in her back pocket when she needs some shit taken care of. That nigga there mean no good. From what I heard, he on folk's paperwork and shit."

"Why in the hell X fucking with him then? She must know all of this if you do."

"She knows everything, so it's beyond me why she's still dealing with the dude."

"Do we need to take him out?"

"Nope. I'll scope him out before we make that move."

Trying to understand X's moves was like getting tar to dry when it's raining; it's fucking impossible. Her moves were precise and premeditated. Before anyone knew what's happened, she's already played her hand and won!

"Are you heading out to your folks' crib for the holidays?" Ruger asked curiously, interrupting my thoughts.

"Nawl."

"Why not?"

"They pissed me off at the funeral, and in return, I pissed them off."

"Whatever your folks and you got going on… y'all need to fix it. Family is very important and precious. No matter what they do, honor and love them," he breathed slowly.

"Ruger, you just don't understand," I tried to explain before he cut me off.

"I know how your mother is. She's nothing to play with. From the way she acts, she wants a better life for y'all then what she possibly had. She's very controlling, and you have to learn how to love and live with her being that way. Sit down and talk to her. Maybe you'll get some understanding of why she's the way she is."

"Nawl, I'm done with them," I replied quickly as I slowly rolled my neck from side to side.

"I won't let you be. I miss my family every single minute that passes. I reminisce about the past just to see their smiling faces."

"Stop reminiscing and visit them, Ruger."

"My parents and siblings are no longer living, and the rest of the family I could care less about seeing them."

I never knew that his family was deceased, and I felt sorry for him because he truly had no one but us.

Not wanting to pry hard, curiosity got the best of me, so I politely asked, "What happened?"

"I don't want to talk about it."

"Maybe it'll help you to tal—"

"I said I don't want to talk about it," he replied, raising his voice.

"Aight, but if you ever want to talk, I'm here for you, man," I voiced sincerely as I turned to see his silhouette.

"Yeah, man."

Crickets were chirping as I let my mind wander on what happened to Ruger's family and whether X knew they were nonexistent. Not able to arrive at any answers about one of my partners, I stood still and transitioned my mind on how I was going to find X.

As I was about to open my mouth to ask Ruger a question, his cell phone sounded off. Eagerly anticipating him saying, "What's up, Chief?" upon answering the phone, I stood tall holding my breath.

"Speak to me, Juvy," Ruger announced coolly into the phone, and I'll be damned if I didn't get mad.

I wanted to walk away, but I had to know where he was at so that I could knock his ass off the map! Ruger was extremely silent on the phone as I overheard Juvy running his mouth. Rubbing my face, I wanted to know exactly what he was talking about.

"Mmm hmmm," Ruger announced.

Feeling jealous by Ruger talking to the dude, I cleared my throat. Ruger didn't turn his head or say anything. He was busy listening to that ancient black beast.

I was relieved and pissed off when I heard Ruger say, "Aight. Tomorrow at four, we'll meet up somewhere. I'll reach out to you about the location. I wanna make sure I'm not being followed."

As soon as Ruger placed his flip phone into his front pocket, I cleared my throat again.

"Damn, something stuck in your throat, nigga? You need something to drink?" he chuckled.

Not finding anything silly at the moment and trying not to sound jealous, I replied in a cool tone, "Hell nawl. I want to know what's going on."

"I'm meeting up with Juvy tomorrow at four. He wants to talk about setting a trap for Reggio and 'nem. It's time for those fuckers to die."

Looking at Ruger's silhouette, I had a quizzical look upon my face as I wondered why he said *him* instead of *we*. There haven't been too many missions where Ruger and I weren't joined at the hip. At that moment, I was feeling some type of way, and I believe that Ruger knew it.

"Go home and get some sleep, Rondon. I know you ain't been to sleep yet."

"Not sleepy. What else did Juvy tell you?" I probed, wondering did he tell Ruger about us fighting at my cousin's funeral— not that I really cared whether or not he told one of my partners.

"Nothing that I already didn't know."

"Damn, why are you closed lipped with me, a nigga you've known since '08?" I stated sternly.

"Just don't feel like talking. I got my thinking cap on."

"Yeah," I spat as I turned around, aiming for my car.

"Go home and spend time with your family, Rondon," Ruger voiced in a genuine tone.

"Nope. Finna go seek X," I replied curtly.

"Leave her alone. She'll come around. Right now she's in a territory that's very sensitive to her... I hope you didn't forget that we voted her out of her own organization. So, she rightfully doesn't want anything to do with us. Truth be told, she can make moves on her own."

"Look, Ruger, X is my woman. Anything she's going through, I should be there. So, I would highly appreciate it if you kind of chill out on the advice. I'm not seeking it anymore."

"If it wasn't for me, you wouldn't have her in the first place. You would still be pushing papers, nigga," he chuckled, which caused me to turn around.

"You act like you want her, and I'mma tell you just like I told that fuck nigga, Juvy... I got her pregnant! She's all mine."

"Go home before some shit pop off between us," he replied in a cold tone.

Knowing that I was on that nigga's territory, I left his residence without dapping him up or saying Merry Christmas. Along the way to one of X's cribs in the center of Prattville, I thought Ruger's behavior was unacceptable. I knew that I had to handle him one way or the other. It seemed like he wanted what I had, and I wasn't willing to give it up. Ruger really had me fucked up, and I was prepared to kill him after I handled Juvy's ass!

Chapter Five

X

Today was Christmas, and it was the first time that I hadn't verbally told my guys Merry Christmas. Each of them texted me Merry Christmas this morning, but I hadn't replied. Call me petty or whatever, but I didn't give a damn. They wanted me off the throne, and I was going to do just that...get the fuck off.

However, I was going to make sure that I was in the clear before I tried to leave for good. Little did they know I didn't need them or any man to help me with the last of my tasks. I truly didn't have time to deal with four men that felt that I didn't know how to handle business.

Being pregnant didn't mean a damn thing to me. One thing I knew for certain, if my first bodyguard, Boint, was still living, I wouldn't have any of this bullcrap going on. He would've removed anyone that thought I wasn't capable of handling my job. It hurt me to the core that my number one goon thought that I was unfit to run my organization. I was the reason why any of those ungrateful sons of bitches were getting money and staying out of prison!

The beautiful, bright sun caught my left eye and instantly, my reflexes caused me to close my eyes as I threw the red covers over my head, causing me to stop thinking about my goons. As the door opened, it squeaked. The smell of bacon and eggs waltzed into my room and through my nostrils. At the same time, Juvy's deep, baritone voice spoke.

"Get your ass up and eat. I might let you lay back down."

"Unh uh, you too bossy for me, sir." I laughed underneath the covers as I pretended to pitch a fit like a toddler by kicking my legs and arms.

"Get yo' silly ass out of that bed, Mrs. Bossy," he replied, chuckling slightly before exiting the bedroom.

Juvy hit me up around 10:00 last night and asked could he hang out with me. I really enjoy his company and vibe, so of course, I said yes. Forty-five minutes later, I was putting in the new code to my little ducked off spot in Clanton—the same one I met Bango at some days ago.

"Get in this kitchen, X'Zeryka!" Juvy yelled.

Laughing, I said, "You better stop calling my name like that, Juvian!"

Throwing the covers off me, I slid out of the bed and ambled toward the bathroom to wash my face and brush my teeth. For some strange reason, I was in a great mood. As I cleaned my face, I was lightly humming a tune that my grandmother used to whistle in the mornings.

"What are you doing, woman? The food is going to be cold by the time you get to it," he stated loudly as I heard him tapping a utensil against a plate.

"I'm finna brush my teeth, sir."

"Good, I don't want to smell that dragon breath. You almost killed me this morning when you whispered good morning. You gorgeous as hell morning, noon, and night, but that breath had yo' ass ugly this morning." He snickered.

Bursting out in laughter, I shook my head and quipped, "You know what? Shit, I don't even have a comeback for that one. You got me."

"I know." He laughed.

I knew then that Juvy was going to have my stomach hurting from laughing at his silly self. Ten minutes later, I was sitting at the dark, cherry wood table. In front of me was a delicious smelling breakfast—cheesy grits, half cooked bacon, well done sausage patties, hashbrowns, perfectly toasted honey wheat bread, and a small cup of mixed fruit. To the right of my plate were a glass of water and a large cup of orange juice. On a folded white napkin was a pink pill. As I pointed at the random pill, I looked at Juvy.

"What is this?" I inquired curiously.

"A prenatal vitamin. Now, take it and eat," he demanded seriously.

With a raised eyebrow, I softly said, "Can I be honest?"

Taking a seat to the left of me, he replied sternly but in a genuine timbre, "Always be honest with me."

"I'm scared of being a mother. What if I'm not good enough? What if I fuck up? What if—"

"You'll be fine. You are well-educated and very protective. Love your baby like your grandmother loved you."

Once Juvy told me that, I knew without a doubt that I could show my child the same type of love that my grandmother bestowed upon me. As I quickly thought about how tender and loving she was, I had one of the brightest smiles on my face.

"Keep those thoughts coming, and you'll be absolutely fine. Plus, I'm not going anywhere."

His comment snapped me back into reality.

"Uh?" I asked as I slid a piece of bacon into my minty mouth.

"You heard me."

As I ate my bacon, I blushed and tried not to look at him. Quickly looking at him several times while eating my food, I noticed that he never took his eyes off me as he ate. Being sober and not in beast mode, I was a little shy. Therefore, I had to break the tension.

"How are you feeling today?" I inquired, hoping that he realized I was inquiring about how he felt about Flema's actions.

"I'm okay now that I'm underneath you," he spoke sincerely.

Nodding my head, I shoved more food into my mouth. The way that Juvy was looking at me spoke volumes. His eyes were filled with lust, and I honestly had to put my pussy on restriction, especially after the slip ups with Bango. I had to regroup and think about the shit that I was doing with him. Verbally, I had to get downright nice with myself. I wasn't going to be sleeping with someone else's husband, regardless of the past. It was just that—the past! Bango forgave me, and I forgave him. Now, it was time for both of us to go on about our business.

"What got you in the zone?" Juvy asked, interrupting my thoughts.

Seeing no reason to lie to him, I told him the truth.

"Finally had closure with Bango. Both of us forgave each other, and I'm okay... I'm finally okay," I stated happily as I looked into Juvy's gorgeous, round eyes.

Nodding his head, he asked, "What about Rondon?"

Exhaling deeply, I replied honestly, "I can't deal with him on no levels. He's too much for me. I don't want... fuck that... I can't be with or around anyone that makes me feel like the uncle I had killed."

"Wow. Rondon makes you feel like Tyke?"

"Yep."

"Have you told him?"

"Yep."

"What did he say? Has he tried to stop making you feel that way?"

"He really didn't say anything about it, and I'm not giving him the chance to stop making me feel that way. The feeling came about after I learned of him fucking around with some random chick. We fought, and he forced us to fuck. Basically, he tried to fuck me into submission. Once I told him that I never wanted him... he grew extremely angry. After he was done handling his business, the way he spoke to me and what he said made me feel like I wasn't shit. Not in a million years have I felt like a piece of ass or had a nigga talk to me the way Rondon did," I announced sadly as I reached for the cup of orange juice.

"I don't even want to know what he said because if it made you feel some type of way, it'll have me ten times as pissed off."

Silence came over the room as the sun shined on the black and gold china cabinet that held the first pair of machetes I'd ever owned. Turning my head to look at the beautiful chrome weapons, I smiled and chuckled lightly.

"I know there's a story behind those machetes."

"Why do you say that?" I inquired while suppressing a smile.

"There's no way in hell you smiling and chuckling at them without a story...I wanna hear it from beginning to end," he spoke eagerly as he stared into my eyes and continued, "I want to know everything about you, woman."

"Everything?" I inquired curiously as my heart began to race and a sheepish smile formed on my lips.

"Everything... beginning with the machetes," he voiced delicately as he pointed to the slayers.

"Okay," I responded as I toyed with my fingers before turning around to reminisce about the first time I ever used my chrome slicing tools on a live person.

September 2004

Looking in the mirror as I applied my first coat of lip gloss to my petite lips, I hated the cute framed black goggles that sat comfortably on the bridge of my thin, medium-brown nose. Since I had my eye exam some weeks back, I dreaded the doctor telling me that I had to have medicated glasses. I didn't want to have my big, brown eyes hidden. It was already bad enough that I had train tracks across my bottom and top teeth. It seemed like after I murdered my sixth victim, all types of shit went wrong—starting with the glasses and braces. Saying that I hated them was an understatement.

After I finished applying lip gloss on my lips, I turned my head from side-to-side so that I could check out my skin. At the sight of the light acne here and there on my face, I grew angry because no matter what products I used, it didn't clear that shit up. Overall, I was a cute looking girl. I had a size 34C breast, a round, juicy booty, and hips that made my grandmother mad. All of my qualities from my brains to the way I looked were a goldmine to my uncle's organization and to my bright future as a Queenpin.

"X'Zeryka Nicole Toole, hurry up and get your ass out the bathroom, so that you won't miss the bus!" my grandmother yelled as she knocked on the door, causing me to stop analyzing myself.

"I'm done, Grandma. I'm walking out now," I replied as I opened the bathroom door.

"Okay," she yelled from the den area.

Knowing where she was located, I ambled there before walking toward the bus stop so that I could give her a hug and kiss. As I walked into the medium-sized den, I noticed my grandmother was sitting on the sofa looking sad. I had to know what was up with her.

"Grandma, what's wrong?" I inquired curiously as I looked into her brown face.

"Just tired, baby, that's all," she replied as she looked into my eyes.

"Are you fibbing right now, Grandma?" I stated in a joking tone, hoping to see a smile spread across her face.

"X?" her soft voice stated.

"Yes, ma'am?"

"I really hope you aren't admiring the shit that your uncle does. I see that you have taken a liking to being underneath him and vice versa."

"I love my uncle, Grandma, but I am not admiring his street ways," I lied through my white, train-tracked teeth. I was past admiring what my uncle did; I was fucking fascinated by the shit.

"X, I love my son as well, but Tyke Toole is not right. I don't know where I went wrong with him. I'm telling you now, do not get caught up in your uncle's shit. I've warned him as well. Now, get out of here before you miss that damn bus," she voiced as she stood and glared into my face.

"Okay, I'll see you this afternoon," I replied, as I gave her a tight hug and planted a kiss on her right cheek.

"See you this afternoon," she responded, as I jetted toward the front room to retrieve my book bag.

Before I left the house, I made sure to tell my grandmother that I loved her. On the way to the bus stop, which was two streets over from my house, I saw Boint sitting at the stop sign on the third street. Looking back to see if my grandmother was standing on the small front porch, I fumbled with my hands. Once I saw that she wasn't, I broke out running toward Boint's 1976 gray Chevy Caprice. As soon as he saw me running, he turned the speakers up in his whip. Within a minute, I was sitting in the passenger seat of his whip.

"Good morning, young buck. Headquarters, right?" his crackly voice stated as he made a right turn on South Court Street.

"Morning, Boint, and yes, headquarters," I replied, as I got comfortable in the front seat by laying the seat back.

Jonathan "Boint" Markson was one of Tyke's men. Upon me entering the organization officially in July, he was assigned to being my right-hand man at my request. He was the best person to guard and teach me since he was a vet in the game. I guessed him to be around the same age as Tyke. Boint was a nice-looking man. He was chocolate with jet black hair that was cut low, sneaky brown eyes with a smile that was to die for, and mouth full of gold teeth. He was six foot three with a muscular body frame and a laugh that made the hair on your neck stand up. It was bone chilling.

That nigga didn't play the radio when it came down to me. There were times he and Tyke had words about me, which never ended well. They would be pointing guns at each other, and things would simmer down once I pulled out my two gold machetes.

"You will not be late to school today, you hear me?" Boint stated as he flew up Upper Kingston Road and jetted through Durden Road, invading my thoughts.

"I know. All I have to do is grab an ounce of weed and three small bags of that Snow White."

"You are taking a big risk of taking that shit inside of them folks school, X," he sighed, taking a quick glance at me.

"I know, but I won't get caught."

"How can you be so sure?"

"Because I don't tell people my business. No one even speculates that I do what I do. Number one rule, you don't be obvious. Rule number two, you don't sell to just anyone. Number three, always pay attention to your surroundings," I voiced before closing my eyes.

"Okay."

For the next fifteen minutes as he traveled the back roads of Prattville to get to Autauga Hill, we were silent. I thought about making money while getting my education. I had a nice clientele at Prattville High ranging from the principal to the fucking P.E. teacher. I never personally hand delivered the products to them. There was always a flunky looking to make money. Therefore, I would pay them to pick the product up from wherever I had Boint hide it at.

When Boint turned down his radio, I knew that we were close to the beige and black manufactured home that actually resembled a real house, which was headquarters. The only thing that took place at the headquarters were personal meetings with the crew and the processing of orders for dope. Dope cooking took place at the eleven safe houses.

Opening my eyes, I unbuckled the seatbelt, dug into the front of my book bag, and pulled out a pair of plastic gloves. As soon as his car came to a complete stop, I hopped out and ran toward my hiding spot. Once I made it to the back of the manufactured home, I grabbed the weed and powder. Hustling back to his whip, I placed my products into another bag separate from my book bag.

"Time to go," I told him as I fixed the gray seatbelt across my body.

Twenty-minutes later, Boint was pulling into the parking lot of Prattville High. Before hopping out of the car, I informed him that at nine-thirty I wanted him to hide the dope by the big oak tree that was in front of the community center. Boint looked at me like I lost my mind. Therefore, I laughed.

"Use your head. Don't get caught."

An hour into English class, I felt my cell phone vibrating in the back pocket of my knee-length denim shorts. Looking up to see where my frail ass teacher was located, I sneakily pulled it out once I saw that she was in the hallway talking to another teacher.

Quickly reading the message from Boint, I instantly became warm. I responded to his text with one word: Beastie. Angrily placing the cell phone back into my back pocket, I started growling. Julia and some of the other fuckers around me looked and began laughing. I didn't see shit funny and my facial expression told them just that.

"What's wrong?" Julia asked me curiously.

"Nothing," I lied.

Knowing that I couldn't leave school to take care of the pain in my ass, I started counting to one thousand. By the time I got to one thousand, I was still heated as fuck.

One thing I know for certain, that fuck boy was gonna regret acting in a manner that I didn't approve of, I thought as I laid back in the desk and let the bright sunrays hit my face.

***

Since school started, my uncle was on a trip somewhere with his latest skeezer. Not here to chastise these bastards, I knew I had to step up to the plate. The crew had been out of hand since Tyke left a week ago. I was downright disgusted at how reckless they were at selling dope, showing off, and trying to start wars with those that we conducted business with. I had to restore order by any means necessary, because there was no way in hell I was going to let those bitches destroy the crown that I wanted on top of my head.

"You think you can do what the fuck you want without any repercussions, huh?" I spoke angrily to Mark.

Mark was one of the runners within my uncle's organization. He was a short, obese, sea turtle looking ass nigga. He had a distinctive gang-war wound on the right side of his face and big, bulky teeth, which I couldn't wait to fuck up even more.

"You don't have the authority to talk to me, little girl!" he yelped as he gave me the evil eye.

"Oh, yes the fuck I do, fuck boy!" I replied, as I punched him in his right eye with the butt of my Cross. As he hollered out in pain, I laughed sinisterly.

"Boint, put that bitch on The Rack!" I demanded harshly.

"Yes, ma'am, Chief."

I watched him snatch Mark up and drag him roughly to a small room that housed The Rack. I loved that device more than I loved my machetes. The Rack was homemade, of course, by Boint. It was a long, dark brown kitchen table that had rollers at both ends of the table. Once the individual was hoisted onto the table, their arms are fastened to a chained roller above their head, and their ankles were bound the same way.

Retreating to my area of the abandon building to suit and boot up for the glorious show that I was about to present to Mark and the rest of the gang, I welcomed the devilish person that wanted to come out and play. Quickly pulling my attire out of a small, black Nike duffle bag and placing them onto the brown folding chair, I was eager to put them on. I peeled off my school clothing in a flash.

After I put on an all-black cat suit, a black pair of calf-high boots with no heel, black gloves, and a gold and black masquerade mask, I looked down at myself and smiled, pleased with my appearance. With the final step left to complete, I hated not having a mirror to look in as I placed my prescription black Sclera contacts in my eyes.

Ten minutes later, I heard the voices of the assholes that I was ready to chastise followed by Boint knocking on the door.

"Aye, Chief, are you ready?" his strong voice stated.

"Yeah, you can open the door if need be," I replied as I shoved all of my clothing into the duffel bag. Opening the door, he handed me a leather cue-like case. A bright smile was on my face soon as I pulled my babies out.

"Happy cutting," I sang to my two gold machetes.

As I walked out of the small area, the men ignored my presence and continued to talk amongst themselves. I was going to stop all of that. I looked at each of the idiots and snickered to myself. They had no idea what they were going to view. They had no idea that I wasn't going to play the radio with their asses. They were going to find out just how the fuck my young ass got down! I had to miss out on cooking my dope to come and get a bunch of old ass niggas together. They acted like they didn't know how to behave. Oh, trust, I was ready to get their ass in check once and for all.

"You ready to begin the meeting, Chief?"

"I surely am," I yelped as I twirled my gold beauties.

Once I was standing in front of the crew, the room started to quiet down and all eyes were on Boint and me. I had to thank my outfit for that. That's why I chose the sexy, controlling clothing. Everyone started taking seats in the brown folding chairs. I hoped that they were a little shocked and worried because they should've been. I had some new changes and a show that would leave them thinking about it until they died. After everyone took a seat, I nodded my head at Boint, signaling him that he could take a seat as well. Once he plopped his tall body into the chair, I began.

"I've called this meeting because it's past due. Y'all motherfucking niggas doing the most, and I don't approve of it.

First off, y'all got the game fucked up if you think y'all are going to conduct business in an unprofessional manner!" I yelled as I looked into each of the niggas' faces and continued, "I don't want naan one of you sons of bitches to ask me a fucking thing until you are spoken to. That rule will stick from here on out. Do I make myself clear?"

"Yeah," they replied in a dry tone. I got real pissed off at how they said it.

"It's yes Chief, to you bitches!" I screamed angrily.

I waited to hear them correct themselves, but they didn't. I heard a chuckle in the back. I quickly walked to the area where I heard the chuckles come from and stopped in front of a Marvin the Martian looking creature.

"What's funny?" I asked sarcastically, staring the funny shaped dude in the face.

"You coming in here acting like you run shit," he replied nastily, looking me in the face.

"Because I do," I stated in a matter-of-fact tone as I began twirling the black handled machete that was in my left hand, as if it was my baton.

Before I knew it, I brought the golden blade down onto his right wrist. The guys around him jumped back as he yelled out in pain.

As I held on tightly to the machete in my right hand, I twirled it around for ten seconds before bringing the golden blade down on the gentleman's left wrist.

He yelped out briefly before dropping to his knees, looking me dead in the eyes and said weakly, "Yes, Chief."

A huge grin was on my face as the other fellas dropped to their knees and said, "Yes, Chief."

"Very well then. I expect not to have any shit out of you fellas, right?"

"Yes, Chief."

"Will you protect me as you protect Tyke?"

"Yes, Chief."

"Very well then. Let me tell you a little something about me..." I paused briefly and continued, "I don't mind killing. I probably have more bodies under my belt than some of you niggas in here. I'm easy to get along with as long as you don't piss on me. I don't give a fuck about family or anyone else that is close to me when it comes down to me getting what the fuck I want. You treat me like a queen, and in return, I will treat y'all like kings. We are a fucking organization; we will work as a team. We eat, shit, and sleep together... well, not sexually, but y'all get what I mean. After an interesting incident that took place last year, it has shaped me into the bitch that I am today, so once again, do not piss me off! Any questions?"

"No, Chief," they all stated in unison as their scary eyes were planted on me.

"Alright then. Yes, this is my uncle's organization, but you will respect it and me. You will act like you have some sense. I will not put up with disrespect or any bullshit. I am going to tone up this organization because it's not to my liking at all. You motherfuckers say you wanna get money, but I can't tell. Running around the city acting like lil' bitches, that's a motherfucking no-no. Ain't no fuckin' bitches up in this motherfucking organization. Either you are going to listen to me, or I will kill you, simply put. You are not going to fuck up my meal ticket because I have improved the way things are ran. Do I make my fucking self clear?" my young voice boomed throughout the abandon building as I looked at each man in his face before walking away.

"Yes, ma'am, Chief," they all replied in unison.

"Please, fellas, do not piss me off. I have a short fuse, and there's no telling what I will do!" I barked with my back facing them.

At the end of my meeting, I had Boint bring out Mark. There was no need in me making a statement as to what Mark did since everyone was aware. Mark thought it was cool to keep money that didn't belong to him—basically, he stole Tyke's portion of the dope money. Once Boint stepped out of the way, I roughly slid both of my machetes through Mark's limbs one by one. By the time I completed the final blow, which was chopping off his head, I analyzed the crew. With fear in their eyes, I flashed them my train tracks and laughed wickedly before exiting the building.

After I finished telling Juvy my story, he stared at me with his mouth wide open, and all I could do was laugh.

"Say something, Juvian."

With a worried look upon his face, he stated slowly, "Umm... well damn... so, you telling me that you had no problems when you cut that man up?"

"None whatsoever. He wanted to act like he wasn't going to show me respect, he thought that I was a dumb young girl, and I had to show them all that I wasn't going to put up with any of the fuckery. The men of this world think that a woman can't hold down a demanding, powerful position whether it's illegal or legal. At the age of fourteen, I had to go hard in the paint, and the only way I knew how to do that was to show people that I loved to kill—even if I didn't."

"Did you have problems out of them again?"

"Hell no. They accepted everything I said or did, especially when I showed them that I wanted us all to win and be well fed. I was loyal to them, and they honored that because my uncle was not loyal to the majority of his men."

"What happened to Boint?"

"He was killed, saving me during a shootout in Montgomery when I was sixteen… right before Ruger showed up."

"Damn," Juvy replied as he grabbed my hand.

Ring. Ring. Ring.

Sliding my chair back, Juvy shook his head and said sternly, "I'll get it for you."

Not used to the type of love he was showing to me, I began to feel awkward but in a good way. True enough, my goons did what I asked of them and so much more, but things were different when Juvy was in my presence. No man I called myself loving brought butterflies, snakes, ladybugs, or ultimate pleasure my way, but that damn Juvy did!

Handing me my phone, Juvy retrieved our plates and walked toward the kitchen's sink. Glancing down at my phone, I saw my cousin, Keithia's, name display. Ready for one of her tales of a crazy night she had, I quickly and happily answered the phone.

"What's up, hoe," I sang into the phone.

"Shit. Cooling. I had to call you about this shit, X," she stated in a serious tone.

"What nih, guh?"

"Auntie Julia on that bullshit, mane."

Not wanting to hear anything about that woman, I rolled my eyes and sighed in a low tone. I was never the type to reject information that I could use.

"What she did nih?"

"The woman saying that she thinks you had something to do with Truk's death."

Clenching and unclenching my fists, I replied before laughing, "What?"

"Yes, honey. She was like, 'I bet that bitch X had something to do with my son being dead. She act like she can't help me find his killer, and the only reason I can think of that she won't help me is because she is the killer.'"

After Keithia relayed to me what our auntie said, I was one laughing broad. Juvy stopped washing dishes and looked at me as if I lost my mind. Quieting down with the snickering, I responded, "Now, why in the hell would I kill Truk? What would I benefit from it?"

"Honey, I don't know. Auntie Julia back snorting powder and drinking heavily."

With a happy look upon my face, I shook my head and said, "I knew it wasn't going to be long before she started back on that mess. Her ass can't stay off that onion. One thing I know for certain, she better stop mixing my name with her dead son. I'mma have to pay her a visit. I'on like being lied on. I don't play that."

"I know that's right. That's a serious allegation to make."

"Sho' is. Who else she said that to?"

"Who knows? It was only me and her when she brought that nonsense to me."

"Where y'all was at?"

"Her house. Momma sent me to check on her since she had just got out of jail for drunk driving."

With a fake chuckle, I stated as I continued to clench and unclench my fists, "Girl, explain please."

I needed as much information as I could get. I never knew when I would need it. As Keithia told me how our auntie was drunk and fell asleep at a red light on Main Street in

Prattville, I had my eyes glued on the chocolate god in my kitchen putting up dishes. Once my cousin was done babbling, I told her that I would call her back.

Gently placing my phone on the table, I sighed heavily before laughing.

Juvy turned around with a quizzical look on his face before asking, "What's wrong with that baby?"

"I think it's time for that baby to pull out the old machetes. I think it's time for that baby to kill again, and I'm not even talking about Reggio and his minions."

Chapter Six

Bango

I didn't get much sleep due to the fact that my father had me up all night talking about X and my marriage. I wasn't hearing anything that he had to say. I was a grown man, and I knew that I was treading on a scene that I had no business being on. However, things weren't settled between X and me.

While we were enjoying family and friends, X only had those niggas that she paid to be on her team. She had family, but her folks weren't family; they were enemies. Her real family was her grandmother— the same grandmother that I killed because I wanted to be in a sorry ass organization led by Big Shawn, which was under Tyke's control.

As I heard my grandmother and Grandma Sue talking, I was very thankful to have both of them in my life. What would I have done without either of them? Shit, probably be like X— not giving six fucks about nothing.

One could say that I was in my feelings since X didn't answer any of my calls last night or this morning. I sent her a beautiful Christmas text, and she didn't respond. I really was hoping to put a smile on her face. When I didn't get a response, I quickly wondered if she was with that fuck nigga, Rondon. Soon as the thought crossed my mind, I surely blew her phone up. After the twentieth call, I left her ass a voicemail. Knowing that once she heard my voice and what I had to say, she would call me back. At 1:00 p.m., I was still waiting on her number to grace my phone.

"Son, may I speak to you outside please?" my father stated in a casual tone as he strolled his tall body into Grandma Sue's living room in an annoying gray and black Adidas sweat suit.

"Only if it doesn't pertain to the conversation that we had previously," I told him as I pulled my phone out of my front pocket, checking to see if I had a text from X.

"No, it's not about that. I just want to talk to you," he stated with a smile on his face.

With a smirk on my face, I wondered what in the hell my father was going to say. No matter what we talked about, it always shot back to X. I was ready for his ass to go back to New Jersey. He was meddling in shit he had no business in.

Hopping up off the sofa, I tucked my cell phone in the same place I retrieved it from and ambled toward the front door with my father behind me whistling. Upon the screen door closing, there was a black Yukon truck with tinted windows parked in front of Grandma Sue's yard.

Quickly looking at my father, he chuckled and then replied, "I have two people that I would like for you to meet."

"And who would that be?" I inquired with a quizzical look upon my face.

As he began to walk away from me, he stated, "Come on and see."

In tow behind him, I prayed that it wasn't X that he had tied up inside. If it was, I was going to air his ass and anyone else's ass out on this lovely Christmas day. Sneakily taking my gun off safety, I was prepared to fuck up everyone's day. As soon as my father was in arm's reach of the SUV, the door opened and out stepped a light-skinned nigga that stood about five feet eleven followed by another light-skinned nigga standing somewhere around six feet even. When the two light-skinned dudes stood side by side, there was no denying that we three niggas resembled each other.

"Dad, are they my brothers?" I inquired in a casual tone.

"Yes, they are," he stated calmly and then continued while pointing at each of them, "Darius, aka Fish, and Barius, aka Bone."

"What's up?" they voiced in unison while nodding their head at me.

"What's good," I told them more so than asking.

With nothing to say, I looked at my father. I was hoping he had something to say because I was fresh out of words. I didn't know what he expected out of me. Shit, I didn't know them niggas. In my eyes, us being brothers didn't mean anything to me.

Clearing his throat and looking at each of us, Reggio voiced, "I would like for y'all to get to know each other. Y'all already know how the Espositos are. With that being said, I want my sons to have each other's back, love one another unconditionally, and always have an unbreakable bond. Is that too much to ask for, fellas?"

The light skin guys replied, "No, sir, it's not."

I had to suppress laughing because those niggas was peeking and seeking our dad's approval. I was cool with the dudes, so I replied, "Sure."

Time passed as we stood at the edge of Grandma Sue's yard, looking around like we were lost. It took my grandmother to come out of the door with her loud ass mouth.

"Bango, Reggio, and guests, are y'all ready to eat or not?"

"Yes, ma'am," my father and I said as the light skin guys nodded their heads while looking at me for official approval.

Laughing at the guys, I stated coolly, "Y'all come on in here. Let me warn you that my wife's grandmother and my grandmother is a beast with that mouthpiece. Whatever they are thinking, they are going to say it. They don't mind hurting feelings. I just wanted to give y'all a heads up. On the contrary, those women know how to cook their asses off. So be prepared to have a full stomach and a severe case of the itis."

"Sounds good to me." They chuckled at the same time my father knocked on the driver's window and told the driver to come back in four hours.

As the driver pulled off, we began to walk toward Grandma Sue's front door. Inside, Donny Hathaway's "This Christmas" was beating from the newly bought black radio speakers that I bought Grandma Sue. As soon as I walked in the door, I started jigging to the song as I placed my eyes on my wife and children.

While doing the Bankhead Bounce to the beat, the grandmothers, Taea, my brothers, and father laughed. Fish did a two-step dance as I danced along. At that moment, I knew that Fish would be an alright dude to get to know. He was silly just like me.

"Marcus, you are truly a bad influence on this young man," my grandmother stated as she tugged on a hideous red Christmas sweater with a reindeer on it.

"Merry Christmas, baby," Otis Redding's voice blared through the speakers.

That was one song that always turned my ass up. I tootsie rolled to the beat with my head up in the air and my mouth puckered like them boogawolves did in the club when they twerked. My folks were laughing from the time I started the foolery until the middle of the song.

"Bango, I can't deal with you this morning," Taea laughed as I went and scooped up our son.

Dancing with my boy in my arms, he had the brightest look in his eyes and the cutest little smile upon his face. Once the song ended, I placed him in his car seat beside his sister. Making an ugly face at Martaea followed by tickling her stomach, she grunted and farted.

Once her sickening smell hit my nostrils, I gagged before saying, "Now, your little tail on punishment for that fart.

You too young to be pooting like that, Martaea. You almost made daddy pass out."

Laughter erupted and Fish said, "She got one of those farts like her uncle—me."

The laughter ceased, and the grandmothers voiced, "Uncle?"

"Yes, ma'am. They are my brothers," I replied, looking at the grandmothers and Taea.

"Well, I'll be damned. Welcome to my home and Merry Christmas, fellas," Grandma Sue voiced happily as she walked over to Fish and gave him a hug followed by hugging Bone.

"Thank you and Merry Christmas to you as well, ma'am," they replied in unison.

My beautiful wife waltzed over and extended out her hand to Fish before hugging him and saying, "I'm your sister-in-law, Taea. It's a pleasure to meet y'all."

"Same to you, Taea," Fish replied with a huge smile on his face.

My loving wife repeated the same phrase and actions to Bone, and he reciprocated the love back. It was my grandmother's turn, and I swear she just couldn't keep shit simple. Her extra ass started in with the pleasantries and by the end of her speech, she hit them with, "Oh yeah, I don't give a damn how old y'all are, but I still whoop folks churren. If Reggio don't like it, he can get his ass whooped also."

Everyone busted out laughing, including me. The thought of my grandmother trying to whoop my tail had me weak. She had to catch me first.

Laughing hysterically with a red face, my father said, "Lord, Mrs. Toot, I'm still in the ass whooping stage?"

"Hell yes. You ain't too old for no whooping," she chuckled before continuing on, "Enough of this chit chat without eating. Y'all go and wash your hands. Shit, I been sipping on that damn concoction Sue made since eight o'clock this morning. That mess got me with the munchies."

Their snickering surely didn't cease from her comment as we washed our hands. Seated comfortably at the table beside my wife and Fish, the clinking of plates began. There was so much food that I didn't know where to begin. On the table sat smoked turkey, honey baked ham, loaded mashed potatoes, green bean casserole, rice and chicken casserole, candied yams, mustard and collard greens, turkey and chicken dressing, ribs, homemade cheesy macaroni, chef styled pasta salad, corn on the cob, potato salad with deviled eggs, and a small dish of cranberry sauce.

"Are we the only ones eating?" Bone asked curiously as he looked at the food on the table.

Laughing, I replied, "As of now, yes. There may be more people coming by later on."

"Maybe?" Fish chuckled.

"Oh my goodness, this table is covered with food. Do you ladies always cook big on holidays?" Bone asked as he began to put greens onto his plate.

"Fourth of July, they go off," Taea laughed before stuffing a rib bone into her mouth.

"Oh wow... am I invited? What do I need to bring?" Fish asked seriously.

"Anything you want," the grandmothers stated as they put some food into their mouths.

We chatted and ate. The vibe was going great until "What Do The Lonely Do At Christmas" came on. My mood went from great to sad. My thoughts were on X, and how she was feeling on this day. The song was her to the T, and I had to reach out to her. I wanted her to know that she didn't have to be lonely on Christmas. I was willing to spend the evening until tomorrow with her. I was prepared to hear the noise from Taea. Excusing myself from the table, I walked out of the front door with my phone in hand. Quickly dialing X's number, I grew upset as her voicemail came on. Ready for the automatic voice to say leave a message, I had my speech ready until I heard my wife's stern voice.

"Are you calling that bitch? Once that song came on, you changed. Your entire demeanor went south real quick."

Turning around to look my wife in the face, I saw that she was truly annoyed and pissed off. Not in the mood to argue with her or anyone else, I replied nicely, "Go back in the house, Taea. I'm handling business."

"I bet yo' motherfucking ass is handling business," she responded nastily.

We played the staring game for a while before she retreated in the house. As soon as she walked through the threshold of the door, I was dialing X's number. Of course, the voicemail picked up, and I was eager to leave a message.

"Please call me back. I've been thinking about you all night and day. I want to spend Christmas with you. I got six gifts for you, and I want to see your face as you open them. I don't want you to be by yourself for the holidays... no holidays at that. X, I just need to be with you. Yeah, I'm with my family, but I'm feeling out of place here. I need us to be kids again. I miss that. This grown-up shit is too complex for me, especially when it involves this current shit. With you—"

I was cut off, since my message was extremely long. Pulling a cigarette out of my Newport pack, I fired it up and prayed that she called me back. Halfway done with my cigarette, my cell phone rung. My heart was racing as I looked down and saw Snoogi's number.

"Fuck," I voiced in a low tone, not wanting to let anyone know that I was disappointed.

Answering the phone, I said in an unpleasant tone, "What's up, Snoogi?"

"Is the festivities popping off yet?"

"Hell yes," I replied blankly.

"What's wrong with you?"

"Nothing," I lied.

"X not answering any of your calls?"

Ignoring his question, I asked, "Where are you?"

Before he could answer, I heard the noise on his end. The same beat of a song that I heard on Snoogi's end, I swore I heard when I took the phone away from my ear. The beat of the song was very familiar. Closing my eyes and zoning in on the sound, I laughed once I knew what it was and who was playing it. Hanging up the phone, I anticipated seeing The Beast stroll down my grandmother's street, but I also knew what type of hell that would be.

Heart on one million, I didn't know what to expect. Therefore, I stood there looking at both ends of the street. The beat of Project Pat's "Flippin N Stackin" was blaring even louder than hearing it from a distance, letting me know that X was in Braisedlawn. The loudness of the car was inching closer to Grandma Sue's house, and my heart was doing numbers.

Topping the corner of Braised Street was The Beast with X sitting on top, dressed in all black. I was frozen in place as a smile was brought on my face. X's whip was cruising down the street as people began to come out of their homes, peeking at the noise maker. Folks in Montgomery knew about The Beast and the mysterious driver that rarely sat on the car while it was in drive mode. The song went off, and X played it again. That heifer began waving like she was Miss America, and I was tickled as fuck. She was putting on a show, and for the life of me, I wanted to know why she was playing during such a delicate time as now.

"I'm flippin'. I'm stackin'. I'm flippin'. I'm stackin'. I'm flexxin'," Project Pat's voice screamed from the speakers as X flexed her muscles.

While her car cruised down the road, my heart felt like it was going to burst out of my chest. When the beat broke down and the rapper rapped his verse, X was inches away from Grandma Sue's house. She sat comfortably on the hood of her car with her legs dangling, a beautiful smile that showed her bottom grill, and a black skull cap was secured over her head while her long, jet black hair was flowing past her shoulder. X was dressed in a tight fitting all-black outfit; a special made black glove was on her right hand—that glove controlled the steering wheel, acceleration, and braking system. Black steel toe boots were secured on her feet. Immediately, I knew what time it was. She was about that life, and I was willing to protect her, my children, my wife, and the grandmothers.

Before X brought the car to a complete halt, the doors of The Beast opened, showing that no one was inside. Project

Pat's song went off, and I'll be damned if she didn't play it again.

Stopping her black on black, trimmed in gold Caprice in front of Grandma Sue's house, X sat comfortably with a smirk on her face as she kept her eyes on the house. I thought the speakers were hella loud, but that heifer turned it up more and started jigging to the song. Before long, it wasn't just X and me outside of Taea's grandmother's house; I didn't have to turn around to know that. The smile on her face as she pointed in the yard informed me of that. With her muscles still flexed in the air, X started laughing, which was inaudible due to the music blasting.

She cut the radio off and announced, "Reggio, I'm flippin', I'm stackin', and I'm flexxin'. Motherfucker if you want me... here I am! You came for the wrong bitch. I don't care what my uncle told you. The number one rule of *my* streets in Alabama is that you talk to the person that you *supposed* to have a problem with. Don't send your fake ass goons to handle a job you ain't cut out for. I'm a full-time beast! If you want me, bitch, come get it! I ain't running. I'm in the city all day. No more innocent people getting shot because of yo' fuck ass! I have no quarrels with Bango or his wife... this shit is all about you and me! If you eager to cease my life... hop in your white SUV over there and fucking follow me!"

"X, leave, baby... leave now!" I told her at the same time I turned my head to look at my family.

Taea was in shock, yet anger was all over her face.

"You might want to listen to my son, darling," Reggio hissed.

"Dad, shut the fuck up!" I yelled while turning my head to look back at the woman that was truly fed up with life.

Webbie's "You Bitch" played on her speakers, and X grinned before turning down the radio.

"You bitch, you bitch, Reggio Esposito, you a bitch nigga! I am not the bad one... I don't fuck wit' people that don't fuck with me. Tell Bango how you sent your crew at us in August of '08... You gave out the order to shoot to kill no matter who I was with. You was willing to kill your son... Now, bitch, move som'!" she yelled before laughing hysterically.

Before I knew it, my father was running in full force past me toward X. It didn't take me long to run behind my dad. There was no way in hell he was going to put his hands on her, and it was no way in hell I was going to let her kill him. I knew what she was capable of; my father didn't know she lived for killing. As I reached out for the collar of his shirt, it was too late. X kicked my father in the face with her feet. The noise that left his mouth had me chuckling slightly. That was the funniest noise in the world. As soon as he stumbled back into me, I held on tightly to him and yelled, "X, baby, get out of here, please. Check your damn phone."

"I'm leaving, Bango. I'm just tired of your father harassing me over some shit I have no clue about," she stated in a calm voice.

"Bitch, you know why Reggio is at your ass," Taea shouted and then continued, "You shot my husband at our wedding day."

"Get your ass in the house! Stay in your place, Taea!" I yelled sternly as I turned around to see that my wife was walking toward X's car.

"Bone and Fish, please grab her ass and make sure she stays in the house!" I barked at my brothers.

"Don't y'all touch me! I'm ready for this hoe! She did the ultimate no-no," Taea barked as she charged toward The Beast with my brothers behind her.

X began to laugh and growl at the same time. She didn't move as she saw Taea, Bone, and Fish coming forward. Not wanting to release my father from my embrace, I was very relieved when Bone scooped up a yelling and cursing Taea.

"X, baby, please go. Check your phone!" I voiced sternly as she hopped off the hood and ambled toward the driver's seat.

"You seriously calling this hoe baby and shit... telling the bitch to check her phone...nigga, you know you finna give me a fucking divorce ASAP. You still got feelings for a bitch that shot you at our wedding. Have you lost your damn mind?" Taea screamed.

Ignoring her, I put all of my attention on X as she opened her mouth to speak, "Bango, I want your father released from your embrace. Make sure that he makes it to his SUV. This shit has gone on long enough. If he's seeking me, he shall have me... all of me."

Shaking my head, I replied, "No. I'm going to protect you at all costs, X. I'm not going to have it any other way."

"Son, let me go so that X and I can handle our business away from your babies and *wife*," Reggio spat calmly.

"No, you are going to go in the house," I voiced sternly as X slid her beautiful body in the driver's seat and slowly drove off.

The next three hours were pure torture and then some. I had to endure the grandmothers yelling at me for what took place, Taea crying and putting her hands on me, and my father roughly talking in Italian. Once I was done hearing the bullshit from everyone minus my brothers, I fled the house and sat on the edge of my grandmother's driveway—smoking blunts back to back with Bone and Fish, while trying to reach X.

After I said that I wasn't going to call her anymore, I did and thankfully, she answered the phone.

"Where are you? What were you thinking?" I fired off in a casual tone.

"Tired of thinking, and I'm ready to get this shit over with. Whatever happens, happens," she replied in a blank tone.

"Lies. I'm not going to let anything happen to you, X'Zeryka. I mean that shit. You and my father gotta talk like two grown people."

"Your father doesn't want to talk; he wants my head. If that's what he's seeking, got damn it, Marcus, I'mma give him a helluva fight for it. I've never been the type to back down from shit!" she yelled before her voice broke down.

I knew it was more going on than just my father seeking her death; it was twelve years of bullshit she endured from her grandmother's death, her uncle, the lifestyle she badly wanted, followed by not having love in her life.

"I love you. I always have loved you! I'm willing to..." I paused before speaking the truth that only I knew since the last time that she and I slept together.

Wanting to reveal what I was willing to do, I carefully thought about it before saying it. She didn't give me a chance to reveal it before saying, "I'm just tired, Marcus. I'm real tired. I will see you around, okay?"

"Where are you?" I voiced sincerely.

"Sitting at our favorite park," she replied before she started crying.

"Don't do shit stupid. I'm on the way," I voiced as I jumped to my feet and took off running toward my Cadillac, which was parked in Grandma Toot's yard.

"No. I need time to myself," she sobbed.

"No you don't. You need a friend, and I'mma be there for you."

"Taea loves you. You disrespected her long enough for me. Leave me be. I won't harm you, her, or your precious kids. I just want your father up front and center," she replied as I opened the front door of my whip and hopped in.

"I fucking love you... don't you understand that?"

"Yeah," she retorted in a sarcastic tone, and then continued, "You're supposed to be love should've found its way when were sixteen instead of now that you are someone else's husband. Get the fuck off my line!" she hissed before hanging up the phone.

Throwing my phone on the passenger seat, I started the engine and reversed my whip out of my grandmother's yard. Rolling down my window, I told my brothers that I would see them later on. While they dapped me up and wished me luck, I saw Reggio and Taea step outside. Not wasting anytime talking to them, I mashed the gas pedal and zoomed off Braised Street.

As I made a right turn onto Mobile Highway, I began to think about the one woman that I was sacrificing my marriage for. Pressing the gas pedal to the floor, I remembered the first time I met X. She was young just like myself. Just like now, she surely was gorgeous back then. She had the brightest smile that made time stop, even with the braces on her teeth; big, brown eyes that were surrounded with dark brown eyelashes that drove me insane, an accent that was not southern, even though she was born in Alabama, and long, shapely legs that were cinnamon brown had me mesmerized.

She was pure brains and then some; anyone could tell just by the intellectual conversations she had with people older than her. At that young age, I knew I had to have her a piece of her if I couldn't have her entirely. I dreamed of us being together when we became older. Therefore, I did everything in my power to make myself seen in the streets. I made it known that I wanted to be more in her presence by requesting to be underneath Big Shawn who was under Tyke and X's organization.

Time and time again, I tried to get her alone, and I failed each time until I grew some balls and stepped to her one night at the movies. She refused me at every angle until I let her know that I just wanted to be her friend. She finally gave in and our conversations were electrifying. I was happy and scared at the same time.

"It's funny that I'm feeling the same way I did years ago… happy and scared. X, I'm praying you don't reject me. I'm here for you," I stated firmly as I drove faster to Cooter Ponds, which was located in Prattville.

Chapter Seven

Taea

I was hot than a motherfucker at my husband, to the point my grandmother or Grandma Toot couldn't tell me what to do. If he thought that he was going to be protecting a bitch in front of my face, he was sadly mistaken. Bango was foul, and I surely let him know just how I was feeling once his ass sauntered into my grandmother's home.

Growing tired of yelling and crying, I resulted to putting my hand on the bastard. I didn't stop until I busted him in his mouth and realized that enough was enough. I was beyond hurt, and for me to continue putting my hands on him wasn't doing anything to help me feel better about our situation.

Reggio and the grandmothers tried talking to me, but I shrugged them off. The only one I wanted to speak to me was the one I was married to. After I walked away from him, the tears fell, and I began to hate myself for not leaving him alone the day X and he had a shootout that paralyzed him for months.

Some hours after the incident, Reggio asked me to come outside. Not wanting to be bothered with him but knowing that Reggio was going to talk regardless, I slowly got up from the bed and slid on my Timberland boots.

My grandmother's home was back to its normal level of noisy. Bone and Fish were holding my children. Before I skipped out of the door with Reggio, I kissed my lovely bundles of joy on the forehead. I told the light-skinned guys and the grandmothers that I was stepping outside to speak with Reggio for a brief moment.

Once we were outside, I saw my nothing ass husband speeding away from Grandma Toot's crib. Anger built up in me because he was not by my side.

Without a moment's hesitation, I stammered, "I guess he's going to be with that bitch."

Exhaling heavily, Reggio replied in his deep, Northern Italian accent as he gently patted my back, "If he does, there's nothing that you can't do about it, Taea."

"Yes, the hell I can! I can leave his ass. Matter of fact, that's exactly what I'm going to do," I huffed, breathing heavily.

"Do you think that is wise?"

"At this point, yep. I've given him too much of my life. That bitch strolling here today shouldn't have happened. The hoe pulled down on us again, Reggio," I cried as I looked at his well-built body.

"Taea, I have put everyone in danger... not Marcus. I'm sure that you know about Marcus and X being involved with one another since they were fifteen or some shit like that. Around that tender age, her uncle, Tyke, reached out to me and stated that she wanted my boy dead."

"Now, you really have to explain that because there's no way in hell that she wanted him dead then or now from her previous statement."

"They were in The W in Atlanta doing what they do best, and I received word that my son was with her. I sent two of my men down there to stop her from breathing. My orders were clear cut... kill her only," he expressed in a low tone.

Wanting to know more about the issue he had with X, I probed further which caused him to continue talking.

"Her uncle stated that X accused my son of stealing $16,000 worth of drugs, and she was going to kill him once she has used him for her personal pleasure. That was the reason why I began seeking her. From her uncle's mouth, X wasn't going to stop until Marcus was placed six feet deep. As soon as I finished talking to Tyke, I was on the first plane down here seeking that dangerous female."

Shit really didn't make any sense to me, because Bango admitted that he and X were messing around until the first shooting took place. Somewhere along the line, someone was lying, and I surely didn't care who it was. Since my husband completely disrespected me today, whatever he and that woman had going on was their business. My kids and I were getting the hell away from the mess he had created.

"Whenever I tried to locate her, I couldn't find her. I warned Marcus left and right to stop dealing with the female, but he wouldn't listen to me. He swore up and down that she wasn't like what Tyke was describing. Taea, I don't know what X has up her sleeve, but she will not kill my boy or destroy your marriage. I can promise you that X will be dead by the end of this month. Do not file for divorce. You'll have my son all to yourself."

Looking at Reggio as if he had lost his mind, I sounded off with a sarcastic noise before walking away.

"Taea?" Reggio voiced lightly.

"Yeah?" I replied, not looking at him.

"Do you want Marcus in your life?" he asked passionately.

"Not anymore," I responded honestly as I strolled into the house.

Grabbing my children, I told everyone goodnight and informed them that I didn't want to be disturbed. After I placed a kiss on the grandmother's foreheads, I skipped off with my sleepy children. I hated what became of my relationship; I hated that we have been married less than two years, and we were still in the same situation as if we were just friends only.

After I laid my children down, I sat on the edge of the bed and rehashed everything that took place hours ago. The way that Bango was staring at the woman made me sick to my stomach. The compassion in his voice as he called her baby tortured my soul. The way he rushed behind Reggio to stop him from putting his hands on her were gut wrenching. Last but not least, the way she glared at him further let me knew that I had no dog in that fight between them. She loved him, and I really believed that he loved her!

I had only one question for myself— what was I going to do? Fight for my marriage and children's father or let him be since he had continued to disrespect me when it came down to females? The answer should've been pretty simple, but my feelings were tied to that man something awful. However, at some point, I had to say when I had enough. At some point, I had to know when I simply lost the battle and move the fuck on.

While I sat on that bed with conflicting emotions, I stared at my phone, hoping it would ring. One hour turned into two, and two turned into three, and I knew without a doubt that I lost my best friend/husband for life.

Chapter Eight

Rondon

By 5:00 this morning, I gave up on searching for X. I was very sure that she was going to resurface. When I made it home, I ran to my liquor cabinet. I had some plotting to do. Ruger surely showed his ass, and then he had the nerve to blow up my phone, talking about Merry Christmas. I hung the phone up in that nigga's face and rolled back over in my bed.

Looking at the platinum circular clock on my kitchen wall, the time read 3:30 p.m. With nothing to do, I exhaled heavily and sauntered to the front room. Upon entering, I grabbed the remote control off the light brown coffee table and flipped on the TV. ESPN was my favorite channel; therefore, I placed my device on the station. Sinking my body into the soft cushions of my black and grey sectional, I stretched out and enjoyed what the sportscasters were talking about.

Ring. Ring. Ring.

Ignoring my house phone, I continued to indulge in the TV. While my house phone was ringing, my cell phone began with the fuckery.

Not in the holiday mood, I yelled, "Fuck! Who is calling me? Y'all don't want shit but to tell me Merry Christmas... fuck this holiday!"

Soon after, the phones stopped ringing, but they began again. For the next fifteen minutes, I ignored the ringing of my devices. After thirty minutes of no ringing phones, relief consumed me, and I was able to enjoy and chime in on what the sportscasters were ranting about.

I was all into the TV, but that didn't stop me from hearing two doors being shut, followed by Ruger's, J-Money's, and Baked's voices in my yard. I had it set in my head that I wasn't going to answer the door, however, all of that shit changed once those ignorant fools started knocking on my door.

"We know yo' funky ass in there... so open up the door, Rondon," Baked chuckled as he started beating on the front window. I was very thankful that my blinds and curtains were black. They would've seen me lying on the couch.

"If you don't open this damn door, I'm going to kick it in!" Ruger shouted before bamming on the door.

"I know the nigga in there, because his car is outside. He need to stop acting like a little pussy ass nigga, and open up," J-Money barked.

"Y'all, come on... if he wanna act like he on his period, then we will let him be. I guess we gotta trail X ourselves, since she just dropped down on Reggio in Braisedlawn," Ruger spat, intentionally, knowing that the mention of X was going to bring me out of my funky mood.

"Y'all fuck boys better not go anywhere," I yelled as I jumped from the sofa and ran toward the door. As soon as I opened the door, the sunrays blinded me before I put my hand over my eyes. Standing in the door with my boxers on, I questioned them.

"What in the fuck was she doing in Braisedlawn, dropping down on Reggio without us?"

"Dude, put some clothes on so that we can hit The Gump," J-Money spat before laughing.

"Mane, I gotta take a shower and all that."

"It's after three, and you ain't washed that ass yet?" Baked voiced in an agitated tone.

"Nawl, I had a rough morning. I tried my best, looking for that girl," I told them as I ushered them to take a seat. As usual, Baked and J-Money raided my fridge and cabinets. Ruger took a seat on the short sectional and didn't mumble a word.

Before I strolled toward the bathroom, I asked him, "Where are you meeting Juvy?"

"At a secret spot," he replied, not looking at me. I glanced toward J-Money and Baked to see if they had an issue with Juvy and Ruger meeting up, and them niggas didn't seem a bit bothered at all.

"So, you aren't going to tell me?" I probed, feeling the hairs on my neck stand up.

"Nope," he responded blankly as he glared into my eyes.

"What the fuck? Why the fuck not?" I shouted.

"Because you are going to start a fight with him the moment you place your eyes on him, and right now, that is not needed. He and I are going to discuss a plan that will get Reggio and his boys far away from X."

Not hearing the noise he was talking about, I shrugged him off and asked the other two guys a series of questions.

"Do y'all trust that nigga, Juvy?"

"I don't see anything wrong with the cat," Baked voiced as he threw a handful of Cheez-Its in his mouth. J-Money nodded his head, in agreeance with Baked.

"Not one time have y'all thought that he was up to something?"

"Nope," J-Money spat while Baked stared at me before busting out laughing. Not seeing anything funny, I questioned him.

"What is funny?"

"You, nigga," he quickly piped and then continued, "You and that nigga competing for Chief. You don't like that nigga, because he had some of her goodies. You in defense mode, dude."

"Wouldn't you be?"

"Hell fuck yes," they replied in unison before nodding their head and snickering.

"So, it's natural for me to be at that nigga's head. I sho' nuff gotta get ahold of him, since he talked that cash money shit at my cousin's funeral."

"Wait! You and this nigga was at the funeral together... in Miami?" J-Money asked as he planted his elbows on my freshly polished brown table, followed by dropping his head in his hands.

"Oh, nigga, you finna spill those beans," Baked stated eagerly as he pulled the barstool from underneath the table.

"Him and Flema were fucking around heavily... of course y'all know that. Soon as dude walked in and I saw him, I was immediately ready to fuck up the funeral. He came over to apologize to my cousin for the loss of her daughter, and I lost it. Next thing you know, me and dude were fighting in the church. Once my brothers and some other dudes at the funeral pulled us apart, he went off on Flema's mother and waltzed off toward the door. By the time he made it to the door, I made sure to tell that nigga that I was going to see his ass again. That black nigga hit me with, 'I'll be waiting while I'm laid up with X.'"

J-Money and Baked were sitting at the table with raised eyebrows as their mouths made the O shape. After what I told them set in, those ignorant niggas busted out in laughter.

Not seeing shit that took place and was happening right underneath my nose funny, I told them, "Fuck y'all. Y'all see everything funny. I'm finna take a shower so that we can hit this road to see where she is. She has a lot of explaining to do."

"She might be laid up with Juvy," Baked joked.

"Baked, I play about a lot of things, but joking like that ain't one of them."

"Shouldn't you be worried about Jacquel's ass?" Ruger shouted, which caused the runts at the table to grow louder. Turning my head briefly to look at Ruger, I made a smirk and walked off on his dumb ass.

Fuck them and Jacquel. She could go to hell for all I care. She and my parents had been working my nerves all morning long with all those questions. I had to put both of them on the block list, and I surely didn't read one text message or listen to any voicemails. There were only two people on my mind, and that was X'Zeryka Nicole Toole and that nigga, Juvian King.

***

There was not a person in the streets that were willing to talk to us about X. Everyone that knew who we were didn't say shit. It was as if we were on the outside. Niggas that feared us were looking us in the eyes as if they were ready to do something. The once intimidating atmosphere we walked in with X was gone. Right then and there, we quickly knew that folks weren't scared of us. They were horrified of X... our Chief!

I dropped Baked and J-Money off at Baked's crib. Ruger was probably still out and about with that cat, Juvy. With nothing to do but go home, I quickly realized that I didn't have any groceries. By it being a holiday, my number two grocery stores weren't open. Therefore, I had to bite the bullet and drive back to Montgomery. The only store that I knew was open on a holiday was Capitol Market, a grocery store that housed all cuisines.

Thirty minutes later, I was pulling into the large parking lot, and I was eager to go home as soon as the smell of raw meat hit my nostrils. As I yanked a cart, I was one gagging ass nigga. I truly didn't see how people were able to tolerate the smell. Fifteen minutes turned into forty-five minutes, and I was still strolling through the stinky store. I guess boredom got the best of me, but the amount of shit I had in the buggy informed me that it was time to leave the funky place.

When I walked out of the front doors of Capital Market, I saw X sitting on the hood of my car with a lollipop in her mouth and right leg placed comfortably on top her left leg. She was dressed in all black, no sleeve cropped top that dipped low in the breast area which were sitting nice and pretty. A diamond studded necklace was secured around her neck with the matching earrings. A matching bracelet was on her left wrist along with the matching ring on her left pinky finger. Black tight fitted, cut up jeans held all that thickness. On her feet were some expensive black high heels. I believe those shoes were Giuseppe Zanotti. Those were some bad ass black heels, and I immediately imagined her parading around her crib with nothing on but those heels.

They had to have been five inches or so, made in metallic leather with two straps around the ankle region, open toe, and a winged out design in the front of the heels. Black designer glasses were propped up nicely on the bridge of her nose, but I noticed that she had on her all black Sclera contacts in. Her nails and toes weren't polished in that nude color that she had on earlier today. They were polished black.

As I approached my whip, I heard X growling like a bear. I wanted to know what was up, so I spoke my mind.

"What's up with you, beautiful? I miss you."

"Growl."

"Why in the fuck are you saying growl on top of growling?"

"Growl," she replied louder.

I walked closer to her and tried to put my hand on her right thigh. With her left hand, she knocked my hand off her thigh, and with the right hand, she sucker-punched me in the mouth. I felt the warm blood in the bottom of my mouth. I wasn't going to lie like she didn't stun the hell out of me, because she did.

"What the fuck, yo!" I spat after I spit the blood out of my mouth. With my fists clenching, I stared at X. I wanted to put my hands on her something awful, but I knew better than to do that.

"Growl!" she voiced loudly as she reached in her back pocket and pulled out a black pocket knife.

"What the fuck is really going on, X? Say somethin' instead of growling... you know I know what that growling mean," I exclaimed with my hands up in the air as I walked backwards, pushing the buggy along with me.

X casually strolled toward me. When she was in close proximity of me, she grabbed my shirt and snatched me towards her—body-to-body. After she glared into my eyes for several seconds, my body was shoved into the driver's door of my car. I was really lost as to what was going on until I realized that something must've happened, or she must've seen something in order for her to behave in this manner. I tried to ask her what I did, but before I could open my mouth, X held the pocket knife up against my throat, all the while applying pressure to it.

"What the fuck, X?" I stated in a low voice. She didn't say anything. She just stared at me with the upper right portion of her lip turned up. It was several seconds before she spoke.

"If you keep coming for Juvy, I'mma slit your fucking throat. You're already running around town acting like you own this motherfucker! Keep in mind... I paid yo' ass monthly, and I'm finna deposit your last payment from me into your account as soon as I leave this motherfucker. Keep thinking I need you, Ruger, Baked, and J-Money... see how this bitch move. I bet you already know how I roll. I heard that you, Baked, and J-Money were out looking for me. Do you see how everybody moves for me and not my goons? See what happens when you talk more than you think, baby daddy?"

After she was done speaking, X released me and slowly backed away, all the while staring at me. All I could think about was putting my hands on Juvy for being a snitch bitch. There was no way in hell I could go up against the most treacherous, dangerous woman that was pregnant with my child. However, I could get ahold of the nigga that was trying to take my place.

"X, where are you going?" I asked in a casual tone while glaring at the beautiful but scary creature.

"None of yo' business. Get you some, and stop worrying about me and mine," she barked, turning on her heels and walking to The Beast which was in front of my whip.

"You are pregnant with my child. You have to talk to me. We need to settle things, X, once and for all."

"Like I said before, come for Juvy again, and we surely gonna talk. As far as this pregnancy, you are not involved. I refuse for you to make me feel like Tyke has all of his life! So, steer clear of me!"

With that statement, I held onto the buggy as she retreated to the driver's side of The Beast. As soon as she slid her body in the front seat, the radio blasted "You Bitch" by Webbie. I knew right then that she was beyond pissed off and was cutting ties with everyone, so I was in deep shit. The entire time the song played, X was revving the engine. One wouldn't know, because the speakers were so loud, but I saw how that front of the car kept going up and down.

Employees and customers of Capital Market looked at what was playing out between us. I tried to get in my car, but my legs wouldn't move.

"You uh bitch, nigga! You uh bitch!" Webbie's voice sounded off before "Move Bitch" by Ludacris played. That heifer sat there in the parking lot and burned rubber until she was tired. Some of the people that were out there looking hurriedly left the scene, while the others continued to see what was going to happen next.

For the first time, I was shook behind her antics, because I wasn't on her side. I was the one that gave out warnings to those that pissed her off. Truth be told, I was downright scared by her demeanor. I really thought that once I got her pregnant, she would turn into a womanly woman. Shit, I was dead as wrong.

As Mystikal's verse blared through the speakers, X flipped the switch on her hydraulic panel, and that motherfucker rose off the rubberband tires. As soon as her car rose, she took her foot off the gas, and that got damn car started bouncing up and down. That was my cue to get the fuck out of the way! As soon as I moved, she rammed into my car, causing it to slam into the back end of another parked car which was parked on a different aisle but within walking distance from my car. She fled from the scene with "Move Bitch" blasting from her speakers as she traveled down the Boulevard.

The airbags popped out immediately after my car settled on the back end of the other car. With my mouth wide open, I stood there shaking my head. I couldn't bring anger forward, because there was no need to do so. I knew what I had done to cause her to lash out at me.

Customers and employees asked me if I was okay and did I want them to call the police. I told them that I was fine and not to call the police. I was going to handle this without the police being involved. I walked to my banged up car, opened the door, and retrieved all of my belongings out of it. As I contacted a towing company, I wrote down my information so that the person's car that was damaged in the back could file a report. I called J-Money and told him to come and pick me up. As soon as I hung up the phone with him, there was an angry customer screaming about what happened to their car. I had to get ready for the upset older, white man.

It took me a while to calm the man down and explain to him what happened without throwing X under the bus. The man didn't want to hear shit about not calling the police. Within ten minutes, a squad car and the towing truck pulled up. He asked me and the white man questions pertaining to the accident. I tried to leave X out of it, but of course, some Chinese woman spoke up about what took place.

"There was this black car... I think the name of it is a Caprice. It had black tinted windows, big wheels with rims on it, and loud speakers. The woman plowed into this gentleman's car, causing the car to hit the back end of this gentleman's car," the lady stated as she pointed at me and the white man.

As the lady continued to talk, the look on the officer's face told me everything... that nothing would be said or done to X. The officer was looking like he didn't want any run-ins with my girl, and I was very thankful for that. When I heard J-Money and Baked's voices, I quickly wondered how in the hell they got to Montgomery so quickly.

As they approached me, the officer told the man and me to exchange insurance information--which we did. The officer completed the report and handed both of us a copy of it. I noticed that he described a black Caprice, but it wasn't X's. He asked to speak to me alone. Nodding my head, I walked behind him as he strolled toward his patrol car while J-Money and Baked were on my heels.

"What did you do to piss off X?" he stated in a shaky voice.

"I didn't do anything, sir."

"You better be careful around her. She is nothing to play with. You have a Merry Christmas, now."

The officer walked off on us, heading toward the white man. I lingered around to see what the officer was going to say to him. After the officer reassured the man that his car would be fixed without a hassle, he told us to have a good holiday.

Once I hopped in J-Money's Yukon, I filled them in on what happened. Baked and J-Money looked at me in a puzzled manner before asking me, "How are you going to get yourself out of the jam with X?"

"I have no fucking idea. Shit, a nigga really scared to say hey to her. We are really on the outs now. She's making moves without our asses. We need to tread lightly, fucking with her. She truly needs her space," I confessed as I slumped further down in J-Money's backseat.

Choosing To Love A Lady Thug 4

I was quiet from the time I spoke the truth until I arrived at my home forty-five minutes later, looking like a sick and sad, depressed puppy.

Chapter Nine

X

After ramming my car into Rondon's, I fled to Prattville to hop into my F-250. I still had some business that sought my attention; however, this particular issue involved a close friend that lived in Autaugaville. With my phone in my hand, I made sure that I had my arsonists do as I say.

"Aye, now it's time for you to handle your tasks," I voiced professionally into my phone as I cruised Highway 14.

"I'm on it now, boss lady."

"Good. I want to hear about it on the news. That's how bad I want it," I replied casually while flipping on the bright lights and bending the steep curve on the highway.

"Your wish is my command," the deep voice arsonist voiced before laughing.

Ending the call, I was eager to reach Barry's grandmother's house. I wasn't going to entertain the family gathering. I was eager to know why Barry didn't execute the plan of blowing Tyke's head off. Since the trip from Miami, I hadn't had a chance to do anything that I was supposed to.

Barry was the first person I was supposed to have talked to, but of course, some shit got in the way. I couldn't properly mourn the loss of Tony. Of course, bullshit found its way to me. Now that Bango and I had gotten on good terms, I felt a little better about my future. I still had to trap Reggio and his boys. With the help of Juvy, that was already in the making.

Turning on the main dirt road to get to Barry's grandmother's home, I smelled smoke which informed me that they had already fired up the pit and were getting wasted. The farther I traveled down the dusty, rocky road, the more people I saw. When they noticed my black on black F250, they began waving. Pulling behind Barry's white F150, I shut the engine off and hopped out.

"X!" Barry's family and our friends yelled once they saw my face.

"Hey!" I yelled back but not in my usual fun tone.

"Your ass finally made it down here," I heard Chuck say from a distance.

"Indeed... I had some personal things going on that took a lot of my time," I voiced as I aimed toward the direction Chuck's voice was coming from which was in front of an old, rusty, brown barrel in the center of Barry's grandmother's yard.

"Do you want something to drink?" Chuck asked as I waltzed closer to him while he held a stick filled with marshmallows.

"No. I came to speak to Barry. Have you seen him?" I inquired as I looked around for him.

"The last time I saw him... he was in the house."

"Okay. I'll be right back," I voiced as I strolled toward the red and white splotched front door.

The stench of cigarettes and weed made me weak to the stomach; however, I had to think past the smell so that I wouldn't vomit everywhere. My white family was having a blast as Sugarland played from the speakers on the cluttered porch. A sea of bodies was swaying from side to side as they sang along to the country music.

Laughter exploded throughout the massively large acres of land. Everyone was truly enjoying themselves. I would've been if I wasn't pregnant or on a mission to see what had Barry's boxers in a bunch on the most important night of his life... the one I paid him $100,000 to do. There was no way in hell I was going to stay long. If I did, I probably would kill Barry and bury his ass on his grandmother's land.

While I was thinking and looking around for him, I was passing out hugs and slanging Merry Christmas around like it was the quality dope that I made.

"X!" I heard Barry yell from the den area.

With a faint smile on my face, I waved and quickly walked his way. In the den, there were so many people in there that it wasn't funny. There wasn't enough furniture for the different shapes of people. Asses were perched comfortably on the arms of the three worn out sofas, on the sides of two rocking chairs, on the dirty, brown carpet, and in the laps of family members or lovers.

Stepping slowly down the four flimsy tan steps, I waved and spoke to everyone. Showing me love by giving out hugs, kisses on the cheek, and saying Merry Christmas, Barry's family was very excited to see me. Once I reciprocated the love back to them, I asked Barry outside. Nodding his head, we walked out of the den's door and into the beautiful night's air. As we walked through another sea of bodies, Barry and I made light talk.

A good distance away from the house and people, we stopped and I asked him clearly, "Did you kill Tyke?"

With the cup to his lips, Barry brought the cup to his side and glared into my eyes. Those small, brown eyes told me all that I needed to know.

"Yes or no?" I probed, trying not to raise my voice.

"No," he replied shamefully.

"Why not?"

"I froze up. I was beyond nervous. Tyke knew something was wrong as soon as I got in the car," he began to say as his voice shook.

"So, you're telling me it's cool to take my money and not tell me that you didn't execute the plans I set out for you to do?" I questioned curiously as the anger grew in me.

"It was nothing like that, X. I swear," he stammered as beads of sweat formed on his forehead.

"All you had to do was tell me the truth, Barry."

"I didn't see the need to tell you the truth once Tyke's brains were splattered all over me and his car. The dude was dead as you requested."

"But not by your hands. Do you know how much shit you could've been in, and I would've had to cover your ass?" I asked with a high-pitched tone but low enough for only us to hear, as I shoved my hands into my front jean pockets.

"I know. I was glad that nothing came up."

"When I send out a hit… nothing comes up. You must've forgotten who I am?"

"No, I haven't forgotten," he responded in a sad tone.

Fumbling with my hands, I was deciding what to do with my high school associate. He knew that I knew that he didn't kill my uncle, so the best thing for me to do was forgive him and go on about my business.

"All is forgiven. The next time… if there is a next… I send you on a mission, the best thing to do is say something… especially if it doesn't go the way I want it. Understood?"

"Understood," he said with a smile on his face as he opened up his arms, and I walked into them. We stood in the back, talking for a while until a deep voice male called Barry's name.

"Yo, I'm in the back!" he shouted to the guy as he turned around to see who the person was.

As soon as he turned around, I slipped six self-made lethal concoction pills into his drink.

The guy started jogging toward our way, and Barry spat, "What in the hell does this fool want?"

Acting like I was interested, I replied, "Who is he?"

"One of my incest cousins."

Not in acting mode, I was tickled to the max, so I busted out in laughter. When the dude approached us, I was still laughing as he spoke to me. The dude wasn't bad looking... a low-haircut, light brown stubble of hair on his face, blue eyes, tall, with an athletic build. Quickly observing the man, I knew that he was on some heavy shit because of the way his eyes were darting from left to right, his manly hands were twitching and moving about, and he wouldn't stay still.

"Do you know where I can find some meth at?"

I knew the bitch was a junkie, I thought as I kept my eyes on him.

"Nope," Barry replied before putting the plastic red cup to his lips and gulped down the rest of his contents.

Yes... drink it all, Barry, I thought as I held a straight face. Pure excitement ran through me as I knew that Barry's lying ass wasn't going to be breathing for long.

"You are a cop, and you telling me that you don't know where the dope at?" the guy stated in a frustrated voice.

"Yep," Barry quickly stated and then continued, "If you don't mind, X and I were having a conversation."

The guy said some inaudible words and disappeared the same way he came. Barry turned around and looked at me.

"I don't have the money that you gave me to handle the job. Is that cool?"

"What money?" I questioned, playing dumb as I raised my eyebrows. Getting the hint, Barry nodded his head and then smiled.

"You are my best friend. You know that? You are always there for me and always had my back. I love you, girl," he stated in a sincere tone.

"That is what friends are for, and I love you too," I told him as I grabbed his left hand and motioned for us to go back to the party.

Lightly chattering, I felt Barry's hand starting to become clammy. I couldn't smile on the outside, but on the inside, I was grinning like hell. His ass would be deceased by the time I sat my ass in my truck.

"You okay, Barry?" I asked him as we made it to the first wave of bodies.

"Yeah, I'm cool. I'm drunk as hell. Shit is spinning," he stated slowly.

"You need to take a seat. Once we make it up the front room, I'll get you a glass of water."

"Okay."

Soon as we made to the front room, Barry passed out, and my performance began. I was hollering for some help and for him to wake up. His grandmother came over and assisted me with getting Barry to the sofa. At the same time, the music stopped. Someone was on the phone with the emergency dispatch, giving them the address. The house was chaotic as people began to pray and cry from seeing Barry in a life threatening situation. I had tears streaming down my face as Chuck wrapped his arms around me.

"He's going to be alright, X. He has to be," Chuck stated sadly.

Forty-five minutes later, a white sheet was thrown over Barry's face as he was declared dead on the scene. Cries erupted from every inch of the house and outside, including from myself. Pretending that I couldn't take any more of it, I informed Barry's grandmother that I had to go home. Chuck walked me outside, and we were extremely quiet.

By the time we made it to my truck, he broke down, and I had to get in the mode and break down with him. Tired of the crying, I had to set his ass straight but in a nice way. After I gave him a great sympathetic speech for our deceased buddy, Chuck kissed me on the forehead and told me to call him as soon as I made it home. Ensuring him that I would, I hopped in my truck and peeled away.

Once I touched down on the paved road of Highway 14, I was one smiling heifer. I had gotten Barry's conniving ass. He was no longer breathing to tell anyone what I paid him to do. He wasn't able to gloat about the money that I paid him to handle a job that he didn't do.

As I traveled the country roads of Autaugaville to reach Clanton, I was eager to see Juvy and hear about his day with Ruger. Eager to be in his presence, I mashed the gas pedal. I was ready to let my hair down and enjoy the rest of my Christmas with him.

Ring. Ring. Ring.

Grabbing my phone off the holster, my heart started pumping faster which caused me to mash down on the gas pedal. Eager to answer the phone, I did so in a proud manner.

"Hello."

"What's up, Mrs. Bossy?" Juvy's deep voice inquired.

"Heading back to Clanton. What you got going on?" I questioned with a smile on my face.

"Trying to get this turkey right, but I burnt the hell out of it," he snickered.

"Turkey?"

"Yep. I was trying to make us a Christmas dinner, but I fucked up the meat. I set the smoker too high."

"Well damn," I laughed and then continued, "I'm glad I got some food from Honey Baked Ham before they closed."

"See… that's why we are a good team. You already knew that a nigga was going to fuck up something, and you were prepared… my girl!"

"Shoot, I can barely cook a turkey. Plus, neither of us bought anything to eat anyways," I confessed as I peeped into my rearview mirrors at a set of lights that were coming close to me.

"How long will it be before you get here?"

"I would say about forty-five minutes to an hour… give or take the traffic," I stated as I focused on the road and the car behind me.

"Okay. Be careful."

"Always," I replied as the car that was behind me zoomed past me. Hanging up the phone, I was smiling like a Cheshire cat. I was ready to act silly, watch a movie, and hang out with Juvy.

Fifty-five minutes later, I was putting the code into the keypad of the black, iron gate. Zooming through the opening gate, I stopped briefly to see it close behind me. Once I was satisfied, I peeled away toward the trailer home. Parking behind Juvy's Hummer, I shut off the engine. As I closed the front door, he was sliding his handsome, chocolate, tall body out of the front door.

"Look at all that pregnant ass in them jeans, guh. Come here!"

He laughed while rubbing his hands together.

"Shut up," I chuckled as I opened the back door to retrieve the food and drinks.

"Don't you pick up anything heavy. You just get the food, Mrs. Bossy."

"Okay, Mr. Bossy," I replied happily as I only grabbed the six bags of food.

When Juvy was close to me, I inhaled his cologne, and that tingling sensation between my legs began. A soft groan left my lips, and he started laughing.

"Hush up."

"Ouuu, yo' ass turned on by the chocolate man," he joked as he snatched up the four twelve-packs of nonalcoholic beverages.

"If you say so," I replied smartly as I quickly strolled toward the trailer's porch.

"You know it's the truth. I'm not going to harass that ass tonight. We are only going to talk, laugh, and have fun... no sex."

"You must be telling yourself that?" I voiced before opening the door. Hell, if he sat too long beside me, I was going to do something to him.

Once inside, Juvy locked the screen and front door. Pulling the food out of the bags, we made small talk. Fifteen minutes later, we were eating on the sofa and chatting like we'd been besties for years.

"How was your day?" he asked, licking the sweet potato casserole off his juicy lips.

"Very productive, and how was yours?"

"Productive... Ruger and I laid out the map for getting Reggio and his boys. What do you think about setting a trap at safe house eleven?"

"Sounds perfect to me," I told him as I picked up the sliced turkey and shoved it in my mouth.

"Well got damn, you couldn't have torn it apart before shoving the meat in your mouth like that, X?" Juvy asked in astonishment.

"Nope. I'm too hungry for that," I spoke, but it came out in gibberish.

Laughing, Juvy announced, "What?"

After I chewed and swallowed a nice amount of meat, I repeated what I said.

"You must haven't fed yourself well today."

"A little snack here and there."

"You need to stop that. You must eat three meals and a snack throughout the day. Your eating habits aren't healthy for the baby."

"I know."

"Then why are you doing it?"

"I dunno."

"Always be honest... remember."

"I have so much shit on my mind that I forget at times."

"Well, set a reminder in your phone so that you won't forget, okay?"

"Okay."

Silence overcame the room while we watched Game of Thrones and ate. I was tired of the silence and the show; therefore I asked some questions of my own.

"Juvy?"

"Yes," he responded, giving me his full attention.

"Do you want kids? Do you see yourself being a good father?"

"Yes to the first question, and no to the second one."

Completely thrown off by his answers, I had to see why he wanted to be a father but didn't think he would be a good one.

"Explain, please."

Clearing his throat at the same time that he placed the black and gold dinner plate on the oval-shaped, black trimmed in gold coffee table, he turned his body toward me and glared into my eyes before speaking. As I looked at that man, I swear my breathing was off. I became hot in the panties, my hands became sweaty, and my thoughts were on us getting freaky.

"I got two kids with Flema's sister, Wilema. I'm a horrible dad to them. I want to be better at it, but my conscious makes me feel so bad for how I carried on with the two women. I feel bad for having sex with Flema's sister while heavily involved in some type of relationship with Flema. Every time I look at those children, I think about how messed up it was for me to do what I did with Wilema."

Hearing him say that he had two children with his ex-thingy sister was mind blowing.

If the chick knew that shit, that was probably the reason why she killed herself, I thought as I looked at Juvy in a shocked manner.

I was not going to touch the topic of how he ended up fucking the girl's sister. Instead, I focused on the children.

"Now, Juvian, you know those babies didn't have anything to do with you and your ways. You need to get to know your children. They are a part of you."

"I know. I want to, but if they ask me questions as to why their mother and I aren't together… how in the hell am I supposed to answer the question? When they grow up and people start to talk, how am I going to answer their questions on why I was such a horrible guy to their auntie and mother?"

"I don't know, but I will be by your side to help you. How old are they?"

"Bryson is six, and Taylor is ten."

"Two boys who are going to be hell just like their dad," I said before chuckling, trying to lighten the mood.

"Taylor is a girl," he replied before laughing heartedly.

"Oh shit... my bad," I stated apologetically.

"Were you serious when you said that you would be by my side?"

"Indeed."

"So, what are we?"

Looking at him with a smirk on my face, I replied, "Oh my... I thought I was supposed to be asking you that question, Mr. Bossy."

"Answer the question, lady," he voiced seriously.

"We are what we are... as of right now, I don't know, but I know I don't want you out of my life. I know that I don't want you in my life as my goon. I'm in the process of letting that life leave me."

"I guess I can deal with that answer," he smiled.

"Are you comfortable with me being pregnant by another man?"

"Shid, how you know that's his baby?" he laughed.

I outstretched on the sofa, laughing from that ignorant nigga's comment. When he first touched back down from Miami, he told me about him and Rondon's brawl. I was tickled to the max by his bold ass telling Rondon that he may not be responsible for the pregnancy.

"You're so petty for that one," I voiced in between laughing as I sat upright and placed the plate on the coffee table.

"All bullshit aside, I'm riding with you and the baby."

"If you are going to ride with me and mine, you gotta make things right with yours and be involved in their lives. I won't have it any other way."

"I'll make sure that they are well taken care of."

"That ain't enough for me. You ain't finna win the best stepdaddy award from me but won't spend thirty minutes with your own."

"Gotcha... soon as this mess is over with Reggio and 'nem... I'll set things right with my kids."

"You better," I replied smartly.

Ring. Ring. Ring.

Ignoring my cell phone, Juvy asked me was I going to get it, and I simply replied, "Fuck no. For what? I'm learning to exit the streets. Plus, I'm in the presence of who I want. Everything else doesn't matter."

"Ruger is worried about you."

"Umph, that's good."

"Reach out to him, X'Zeryka."

"I will... but not tonight," I stated in a fake Bernie Mac voice, which caused him to laugh.

Ring. Ring. Ring.

Grabbing my phone off the end of the sofa, I saw that Bango was calling me. It took everything in me not to answer the phone. As I inhaled deeply, I powered off my phone, ready to enjoy my night with the one man that I never thought I would be enjoying it with.

Chapter Ten

Juvy

I was one happy nigga as X lay in my arms. There was no other place I'd rather be than underneath her. She was a well-trained killer and an excellent dope maker and seller, but nothing compared to how smart and wonderful she was. I wouldn't change anything about her. The more I picked at who she was, the more interesting she became. Not wanting to watch another episode of Game of Thrones, I reached for the remote control, flipped off the TV, and spoke gently to X.

"Let's go and take a nice, hot bubble bath."

"Oouuu, sounds good to me," she replied as she peeled herself away from my arms.

"Go get that ass tub ready," I commanded before licking my lips.

"Your wish is my command, Mr. Bossy."

As she skipped off to the large-sized gold and dark brown garden tub, I retreated to the kitchen. As soon as I passed the golden threshold of the kitchen, my first stop was to retrieve two wine glasses. After I had them in my hand, my next stop was to the fridge to retrieve the sparkling apple juice and the Moët bottle.

While I was walking to the bathroom with the items in my hand, I heard X singing. That woman had the most beautiful voice. I stood at the door listening to her, and I felt the warmth in my heart for the woman. I felt myself growing more for her. The intensity of the song, I felt through her delicate but firm voice.

As she sang, X began to strip out of her clothes. I was standing on the outskirts of the door like a peeping Tom. I was ogling her goodies as I saw beautifully cinnamon-brown skin. My man started to rise, and that was my cue to waltz in and plant little kisses on her neck.

"Hmm, that feels wonderful and all, but I thought you said no sex," she groaned as she turned around to face me as I held tightly to the apple juice, Moët bottle, and wine glasses.

"All I did was kiss you, Mrs. Bossy."

I snickered with a sneaky look upon my face. Grabbing the items out of my hand, X gave me the 'fuck me' eyes. I laughed and nodded my head before dropping kisses on her forehead and walking out of the bathroom.

"Where is your ass going, Juvy?"

"You'll see. Now get that ass in the tub!"

Running to the refrigerator to retrieve the cheese and fruit tray that I made, I almost fell and busted my tail. Thank goodness I had a handle on my balance. Chuckling at my goofy self, I opened the fridge door, grabbed the items, and quickly peeled back to the bathroom. Upon the entrance to the bathroom, the lights were off, but X was in the process of lighting a thousand damn candles.

With a huge smile on my face, I asked, "How in the hell did you put these candles out that fast?"

"Drop and go... drop and go."

She laughed while lighting the wick quickly. Never been the romantic type, I sucked in the ambiance of the bathroom and X. My body started to relax more, my hormones were back on the rise, and I was one man who was ready to make love and be made love to.

While X continued to light the candles that she placed around the tub, I was setting up our fruit, cheese, and beverage tray.

Wanting to see how far she was willing to be by my side, I asked nicely yet seductively, "X, will you help me out of my clothes please?"

"My pleasure," she informed me in a sexy tone before lighting the last candle and walking over to me.

She took her time stripping my clothes off me, starting with my boots. When she unzipped my belt, unbuckled my pants, and slowly pulled them down, her eyes were locked into mine. I made my dick jump, and she giggled. Sliding upwards, X ran her hands across my upper torso at a snail's pace. Shivering at her delicate touch, I bit down on my bottom lip. Our eyes locked into each other's. I felt the tension and passion that was coming forth between us. With my shirt over my head, I yanked it off, threw it on the floor, and picked X up by her thick thighs.

"May I kiss you?" I breathed against her lips.

"Yes," she responded softly.

Going in for the kill, I stuck my tongue in her mouth and devoured her tongue and moist, hot mouth. I took my time exploring the sweetness of her long, thick, pink fleshy muscular organ. Her passionate groans filled my mouth, and my dick grew harder.

As she started slowly grinding on me, my badly scarred hands were palming and massaging that round butt of hers. X reached behind her thighs, tenderly grabbed my man, and rubbed him against her clit. The heat from her snatch let me know that she was more than ready to receive him. Not wanting to rush anything between the two of us, I removed my tongue out of her mouth and spoke sternly.

"Nawl, Mrs. Bossy. We are enjoying each other's kisses."

"Aw," she pouted as she tried to stick *him* inside of her.

Removing her hand, I began to step toward the tub. As I planted my right foot into the nicely hot bubbly water, she was doing a number on my neck. The tingling sensations went through my body, and I didn't know what to do other than groan.

"You like that?"

"Yes."

"Well, you can't get no more until you give me what I want," she voiced lightly with a smirk on her face as she bucked her eyes.

"In due time, Mrs. Bossy... in due time," I told her as I eased our bodies down into the water and then continued, "We are going to enjoy this little tray I prepared while we talk and laugh. Understood?"

"Understood," she pouted. As I began to pour Moët into a flute for myself, X was glaring at me quizzically.

"What's on your mind?"

"Your dick is extremely hard. How in the world are you able to hold your actions back like that?"

"Try not to focus so much on it."

"I'm horny as hell, and I can barely stop myself from raping you in this damn tub. You sitting up in here looking like a delicious chocolate cake, and all I want to do is enjoy my slice."

"You will... when the time is right. We are going to relax and chat a bit," I told her as I filled the second flute with apple juice.

I knew she was impatient, and I was teaching her that patience was a virtue. She was going to learn to control her urges. That was one thing I noticed about her. She wanted things when she wanted it. I was cool with that, but I wanted to get to know her more. It would help me deliver my loving to her just right.

"So, X'Zeryka, tell me something about yourself that you haven't already told me."

With a crazy look upon her face, I shook my head and brought my head forward, signaling for her to answer my question.

"I am a talented individual, outside of the illegal activities that I'm involved in. I have a community center for African-American youths in three different regions in Alabama. I'm all for the youth not being in the streets. Yes, I know that is kind of a hypocritical statement. Yes, I have made and sold dope left and right since I was fourteen... granted that I learned the different sizes and amounts of drugs by my thirteenth birthday. Yes, at times, I do enjoy killing. Truth be told, it was never my intentions to become a Queenpin and killer. I wanted to be a ballerina that was in musicals and featured on Broadway. This life I led since I stopped being in someone's dance room was not what I really wanted out of life."

The look on my face when she told me that she wanted to be a ballerina was priceless. I would've never known that. One would've never thought that she had community centers for African American kids. That really made me love her more, especially given who and what she was.

"When did you fall in love with the dope world?"

"When I first saw how people were respecting my uncle, the shopping sprees he took me on, and not to forget the nice spring break and summer vacations. I was intrigued by the smell and manufacturing of drugs... all types, from prescription pills to meth. I was about twelve then, but I fully wanted it at the age of thirteen."

"Prescription pills... I must know more about."

"I can make it. It's really simple, truth be told," she chuckled.

"Shittin' me. I tried and failed miserably."

"You are not a chemistry type of guy."

"You gotta show me this."

"If I show you, you will not be selling it. If I'm leaving the game, I don't want someone that I'm involved with to be in that lifestyle."

"Understood... I don't want that lifestyle anymore anyways. I want something regular... a simple nine to five," I stated as I ran my hands through her hair.

"Anything else that you want to know?"

"How did The Savage Clique really come about?"

"After my first bodyguard, Boint, was killed, Ruger came out of nowhere and ordered Tyke to place him with me, which was in May 2006. The following year, Rondon fell in my lap, thanks to him being in every place just for me to look at him. In 2008, I snatched Baked, J-Money, and Silky Snake,

God rest his soul, from under Tyke's hold. He wasn't treating them right, and they had wonderful skills that I knew I had to have on my team. Tyke threw DB on me in 2008 so that he could watch me, which I later learned right before I killed DB."

"What happened to Silky Snake, and why did you kill DB?" I asked curiously.

As she told me that happened to two of her goons, I was amazed at the story behind each of those cats. I was even impressed with her being comfortable for telling me. I knew then that she trusted me with everything, and I honored that!

Once she was done talking, I shoved my tongue in her mouth and maneuvered my fingers in her twat.

"I was enjoying our talk, sir," she replied in my mouth.

"I know, but you told me some valuable shit… meaning you trust me, and for that, I'm ready to give you all of me. It's time to feed the little one," I voiced lightly as I kissed her and kept my eyes locked in on hers while she reciprocated the passionate kiss.

Lifting her bottom up, I brought her down on my hardened man and told her nice and nastily, "This yo' dick now. Handle your business."

"With motherfuckin' pleasure."

Chapter Eleven

Bango

Tuesday, December 26th

Taea was at her grandmother's house, and she meant she wasn't going to plant her eyes on me. I went over earlier this morning to spend time with my babies, and Taea was not present. The grandmothers were, and they scolded my ass. That anger they possessed for me turned Taea's way, after they told her some nice nasty things. She dragged her ass in the living room, quiet as ever. I knew what was on her mind. From time to time, I overheard her mumbling the same thing,

"I guess the bitch won't talk to yo' dumb ass. Well, she better, because I'm not finna say shit to you. It's over."

After she was done talking to herself, she would look at me and shake her head. No matter how many times I tried to talk to my wife, she wouldn't say a word, so I left her alone. Growing tired of her repeating the same damn thing, I hopped up and handed her our children. Once I told her that I would be back later on to get them so that she could have some time to herself, she snapped.

"You think you finna have my kids around that bitch... you are sadly mistaken. If you want to see them, you know where that ass will be sitting while you are in their presence."

"Aight," was the only thing I said before I softly let Grandma Sue's screen door close.

Now, I was sitting on the bed of my childhood bedroom looking crazy. It was one rainy day, and the quietness of my grandmother's home was killing me. I had no one to talk to, and X refused to answer her phone. Whenever I got my hands on her, she was going to be punished the long way. I was going to let her know just how pissed off I was at her.

Yesterday, I didn't get a chance to give her the gifts. By the time I arrived at Cooter's Pond, she was already gone. It was the day after Christmas, and I was still hot at her. All I wanted to do was show her that I loved her and cared about how she was feeling, on a day that she was supposed to be hanging out with family and enjoying their love. When it came down to X and me... past and present... it was never about sex. It was more about relaxing, enjoying life, and the little things without any drama or having to worry about my personal issues.

There was no need for me to be on pins and needles around X. Things came natural to me when I was around her. I still couldn't believe that I was dumb enough to let her get away at such a young age, and I was equally dumb for bringing Taea into my world as my wife, knowing how I really felt about X. Through all the shootouts, fake plots to get together, and wedding fiasco, X'Zeryka Nicole Toole was the one that shut shit down. I didn't think about anything other than pleasing her. She was truly my other half. With Tyke being dead and us expressing how we felt about each other when we were younger, I really believed that we had a great chance of being more than friends and sex partners.

Rondon was no match for me, so I wasn't worried about him at all. However, my father was going to be the issue. He was hell bent on killing X, and I wasn't going to let that happen, because he was lied to and too stubborn to further investigate things himself.

At that moment, as the thunder sounded off and the rain harshly dropped on the rooftop, I realized that I was willing to lose Taea as my wife and best friend for the one woman that I had tried to get out of my system for years. Both of them had mad love for me, and I for them. However, I had more love for X than I did Taea, despite the roller coaster ride that X sent Taea and me on.

Marcus!" my father yelled, interrupting my thoughts.

"What do he want?" I asked aloud as I hopped off the bed and waltzed into the front of my grandmother's home. When I landed in his presence, I glared at him without speaking.

"You need to make things right with your wife. The way you ar—,"

"She's my wife... not yours. Last time I checked, you don't even have a girlfriend. You have baby mamas, so please keep your advice to yourself. Whatever Taea and I got going on is our business," I replied sternly.

"Well... since you put it like that... if you are in the way of me killing X tonight, I won't have any sympathy for you."

Laughing hysterically, I said, "I won't have any sympathy for you if you touch a single hair on her head, Reggio. I don' told you plenty of times about that one. She is off limits. Leave shit alone. If you were a great dad like you are pretending to be... you would fucking listen to me. Is your ego hurt that she ran through your guys... the same guys that were actually in the military and trained just like she did... as a fucking civilian? Or is your hidden hatred for Blacks coming out?"

"Watch your tongue, boy!"

"I'm a grown ass man, dude, so don't address me as no fucking boy. It's either Marcus or Bango. Ain't no boys here but the ones you created from another woman."

"I'm going to respect your grandmother's home and land... if I catch you around that bitch, X... you will have the same fate. Sometimes, you Blacks just don't appreciate shit. What is wrong with you niggers? The only nigger that I know in compliance with me is your grandmother and those bastard boys' mother!"

Right then, all I saw was red. I tore up my grandmother's kitchen and dining area by the slinging of my father's body on the kitchen table. Pots, pans, and plates were on that nigga's head and body.

There was a strong tussle between us, until my grandmother walked in screaming, "Reggio... Bango, what in the fuck is going on? Stop it before you kill him, Bango! He's your father!"

Not hearing anything my grandmother had to say, I tightened the grip on my legs so that my father couldn't go anywhere. As I had Reggio in a chokehold, all I thought about was him disrespecting my grandmother. She was nobody's got damn nigger!

She was yelling at me at the same time Reggio was struggling to say, "Listen to your grandmother," followed by weakly chuckling.

That was the ultimate no-no. He was making fun of her while she was defending his useless ass.

"Bango, whatever Reggio did... it's not worth it, baby. Let him go so that he can get away from my home," she pleaded with me.

"If I let him go, he will do the one thing I asked him not to do. He won't stop being the asshole that he is," I confessed as I briefly looked at my grandmother.

"Forgive him, bab—,"

"Grandma, go to my room, and grab my cell phone please."

She heard the urgency in my voice, and she skipped down the hallway toward my room. While she was gone, I was applying pressure to my father's neck. I wanted his ass passed out by the time I delivered him to X. When my grandmother was in close proximity, I told her to press and hold down on the number two button. After she was done, her shaky hands were holding the phone out to me.

"Put it against my ear, please," I told her lightly. I prayed that X answered her phone. I was ready to get this shit over and done. I no longer wanted Reggio breathing. He was one disrespectful, ungrateful bastard.

"Hello," X breathed sleepily into the phone.

"Where are you so that I can hand deliver this fuck nigga, Reggio, to you?"

"Wait... what?" she asked, dumbfounded. I repeated myself again, and she growled.

"Clanton... the spot."

"I'm on my way," I voiced before I moved my head, signaling my grandmother to move the phone. By the time my grandmother stood tall, I relaxed my legs and roughly pushed Reggio's body off me.

"Where are you going with him?" my grandmother asked in a low tone.

"To some people that should've been killed his racist ass. If anyone asks about him, say you saw him earlier and that he left. Don't say anything else, Grandma."

"I won't, but rest assured... when your ass returns, we are going to talk about this person that I'm looking at right now."

"Yes, ma'am," I replied as I dragged my dad out of the den's door and into his Suburban. Quickly running to my car, I opened the back door and grabbed the six items that I purchased for X. Whether she knew it or not, she was going to accept what I bought her. It came from the top and the bottom of my heart!

***

On the way to Clanton, Reggio's bitch ass woke up, and I sucker punched him back out. I wanted him unaware of where he was. When I was ready for him to be awake, the lovely lady, X, was going to make sure she had his full attention.

When I arrived at our old spot in Clanton, I wasn't expecting another vehicle to be in the yard. I was eager to know who the hell was in the trailer with her.

When I rang her line, I asked her in an agitated tone, "Whose Hummer is that parked in front of the trailer?"

Ignoring what I asked her, X replied in that bossy tone of hers before hanging up the phone, "The code is my birthday."

My hands were twitching, attitude was nasty, and my nose was red. A nigga was pretty angry by her nonresponse. Twenty minutes later, I was still hot as I stared at a tall, dark-skinned nigga by the name of Juvy. From the hickeys on both sides of her neck, I knew that she gave him some pussy.

As I glared at the dude, he was staring right back at me. Neither of us said a thing... just looked at one another. X was in the kitchen, fixing a bowl of oatmeal. I assumed she was waiting on her goons to arrive, so that she could handle Reggio properly.

"I got one question," the burnt nigga stated aloud with his eyes glued on me.

"What's that?" X asked with her back turned away from us.

"Why in the hell this nigga bring his own father to you? Don't you think it's kind of weird that he would do that?" he asked as he rubbed his hands together.

"I brought my fuck ass dad here, because he deserves to be here. Regardless of what X and I did to each other, I love her, and not naan nigga gonna put his hands on her the wrong way!" I spat, standing up as I clenched and unclenched my fists.

"What did your father do that pissed you off so badly that you are willing to see him die?" the guy probed.

"That's none of your business," I replied curtly. I was going to continue my speech, but black ass popped off with, "Whatever is X'Zeryka's business is mine, fuck nigga!"

There was no need in me going back and forth with a nigga that didn't hold a title, so I lunged for the cat at the same time he landed a punch to my stomach. The brawl between the two of us began. I wanted his head on a platinum platter, by any means necessary.

"I know fucking well y'all ain't messing up my spot, Juvy and Bango!" X yelled. I heard a dish drop as she stomped our way.

As we were on the floor, tussling and throwing punches, X cocked a shotgun back, and both of our bodies went limp as we looked at her. She had that *bitch don't fuck with me* facial expression secured tightly on her beautiful face.

"Neither one of y'all touch each other, understood? Neither one of y'all better not say a motherfucking word to the other, understood? Neither one of y'all better be worried about the next, understood? Bango, get yo' ass on the short sofa, understood? Juvy, get yo' ass to the kitchen table, understood? Both of y'all know that I will shoot y'all asses. Do not fuck with my ignorant, hormonal, mentally ill, pregnant ass!"

It was apparent that neither of us wanted any problems with X, so we did as she commanded. I was still heated, but I had to calm that shit down, or that boss bitch was going to calm me down. I never kept my eyes off that dude. I wanted him to know that I didn't like him.

"Now that I got some act right out of y'all asses..." X voiced calmly before smacking her lips and then continuing, "...Bango, why did you bring your father to me?"

Turning my attention away from black boy, I planted my eyes on her face and told her what took place between Reggio and me. Once I was finished, she was shocked at what I told her.

"Well damn... Um, shit... I'm surprised that you didn't kill him yourself," she replied as she waltzed over to the black, short sofa I was sitting upright on.

Taking a seat inches away from me, X rubbed my arm and replied softly, "You do know that he's out for me, and it has nothing to do with me shooting you or even being involved with you. Your father was and probably still is involved with extortion of Kingston, Jamaica's gems and golds. He was responsible for the slaying of a village in 2005 down there. Juvy and I are the last ones that know about it, other than the people your father employs. I need you to find out if anyone else knows about your father's deeds. If they do, we will have to kill them as well. All leads must be closed. I want a happy ending with this baby that I am carrying, Bango. I'm ready for the life I should've been living."

"Actually, X, we aren't the only ones that know about the 2005 slaying," Juvy's deep voice spoke.

"What do you mean?" she probed as she glanced at him.

"My partners, Bone and Fish, and their mother know about what happened. Their mother, Darlene, was the one that told Reggio about the gems and golds of Kingston, Jamaica."

Upon hearing my half-brother's name, I began to lightly chuckle and shake my head. X and black boy looked at me like I lost my mind.

"What is so funny, Bango?" X inquired with a raised eyebrow.

"Bone and Fish are my brothers."

"Wait a damn minute, nih...," X began to say but didn't say anything after that.

"Yep. I'm not the only child as I thought. I met the jokers yesterday. They were the ones running behind Taea."

"I knew who they were when I saw them. I also wondered what in the hell they were doing with Reggio," she stated casually and then continued, "Juvy, did you know they were Reggio's kids?"

"Yep... the day you and Rondon dropped me off at The Warehouse, I was going to torch the building. Therefore, I walked inside. Behold... Bone, Fish, and their mother. They told me things that I did and didn't want to know before that fuck ass nigga, Reggio, hit me in the back of my head."

"Why are you just now telling me that he put his motherfucking hands on you, Juvy?" X yelped as she hopped off the sofa, aiming for Reggio.

"Because you had enough going on, and I wanted him just as badly as you did. I want to be the one to put a bullet in the nigga's head. He's the one that okay'ed for my family not living."

Hearing how much shit that my dad was in made me sick to my stomach. He was a true monster for no damn reason. *He had money, and that was the least of his worries, so what was the ultimate reason why my father was extorting people from Kingston*, I thought as I watched X slap spit from my father's mouth.

"Wake yo' bitch ass up, Reggio!" she sang angrily yet beautifully.

My dad slowly started to open his eyes. He was taking too long to become conscious, so X slapped his ass woke... the final blow. He was up, looking crazy with a wobbling head.

"Welcome to the show, Reggio Esposito. You are tied up and stripped down to your boxers. Now, in attendance today is your son, Bango, and an individual that you tried to use to get to me, Juvy. Is there anything that you need to get off your chest?"

"Fuck you... you bitch," my dad stammered.

"Watch your—," I began to say. I rose from the sofa, but X wagged her forefinger at me.

"Oh no, Bango. Don't do that," she chuckled lightly while staring at my father.

Continuing, she said, "I want him to say those nasty things so that while I'm cutting off a toe or finger, I can remember the horrible, nasty words he spat at me."

"You are one dumb son of a bitch, Marcus," my father yelped at me.

Growling, X sucker-punched Reggio in the face. Blood splattered across his face and the front of her white shirt. Ensuring to gather a lot of saliva in her mouth, X squeezed my dad's cheeks together. Once they were opened, she roughly spat her mucous down his throat.

Instantly, I gagged while she laughed and replied, "Bango, you still have a weak stomach?"

"Hell yes... I hate when you do that."

"If you are wealthy, Reggio, why would you extort the people of Jundo's Village?" Juvy's heavy voiced breathed.

Intrigued by the question he asked, I made sure to pay attention to my father's answer.

"Because if I didn't, I'd be dead. My father is nothing to play with," he replied as he gazed into my face.

"So, your father was the mastermind behind my family and others dying?" Juvy questioned.

"Somewhat."

"Who else?" Juvy announced loudly.

"Myself," my sorry ass dad voiced coolly.

"Did your father want the people murdered also?" I inquired, curiously.

I'd never called my father's father grandfather. Shit, that guy didn't know about me. Hell, he hated all blacks, and I didn't want to be associated with anyone like that.

"He didn't give a damn about Black people, so that decision was solely on me."

"If you had that decision to make, why did you make it?" Juvy probed as he clenched and unclenched his hands.

My father didn't answer the question. Instead, he looked at me.

He wanted to kill them. My father is racists after all. He says he's not, but he gets a thrill out of killing those that aren't light-skinned and White, I assumed to myself.

"Answer the question, Reggio," X voiced calmly before walking to the black refrigerator and pulling a set of cutting pliers off the top of it.

"I was in a killing mode that day. I wasn't feeling too well, and I wanted someone to pay for how I was feeling."

"That sounds like some racists shit to say, Reggio," I commented as I shook my head.

"Look, I found out about the lands based off how smart y'all little fuck toy, X, is. I gathered the right type of men based off y'all little fuck toy, X's, knowledge. Everything I did was based off how fucking smart y'all little fuck toy is!" my father yelled before laughing.

He made sure to put emphasis on little fuck toy, which made me angry. His entire comment on top of the laughter pissed me and Juvy off. Before X could reply, we were whooping my father's ass. We stomped that nigga out. It was one thing to tell the truth, but it was another to insult the one person that was in the mess because of him.

"That's enough, y'all. I swear y'all be moving too quickly. Get the answers, and then you do what you want to do. Bango, you are very hot headed today. Why?" X asked casually as she strolled toward us.

"He and Tyke have fucked us from the very beginning. They destroyed you without you even knowing... well... until it was too late. I wouldn't be married to Taea nor even have children with her if my dumb ass dad and your stupid ass uncle would've stayed in their place. You would be mine and mine alone," I finally confessed as I glared at the man that I hated seeing the sight of.

With my revelation out in the open, X looked at me in a way I wished she hadn't. With anger soaring in me as past images of me thinking about the life I wanted with X appeared, I pulled out my gun and yelled, "Fuck it, man," as I unloaded the entire clip in my father's head.

Once the smoke cleared from the barrel, I had tears streaming down my face as I looked in X's face.

"Bango, let's go outside and get some air," she said softly as she grabbed my gun and stuck it in the back of her pants.

"Nawl, I'm good. I'll clean this shit up. You still have that trunk you put bodies in, right?"

"Yeah, it's in the second bedroom," she replied calmly with shaking hands.

"X, go lay down. You don't look too well. Bango and I can handle the cleanup. I pretty much know what you like, and from the looks of things, Bango knows how to do it," Juvy voiced lightly as he walked up to her and planted a loving kiss on her forehead.

My heart was ripping at the sight of him being the man that she needed. My soul was crushing as I stood there and watched her look into his eyes, the same way she used to look in mine and nod her head. My only chance of making things right between the two of us was fucking dead. All of my cards were laid out on the table, and they were useless.

We watched her walk off and wipe the tears away from her face.

Juvy glanced at me and said, "Ready to get this over with?"

"Yeah," I replied in a dry tone.

As we walked down the hallway to the second bedroom, there was tension between us. I avoided looking him in the face, even though he kept his eyes on me.

Growing annoyed with him staring at me, I finally stated, "What dude?"

"Out of all the shit that went down between the two of you, you still love her?"

"I never stopped loving her. I never knew that all of the shit that she went through was because of her uncle and my dad. She's not a bad person. She really isn't. I learned a lot about her character after she shot up my wedding. After I healed, I snuck back into Alabama... on a mission to kill her, and I found out a lot of things," I voiced before exhaling while lifting up the chest.

"I was told that she was the reason behind my family being murdered, and I still hung around her. For a while, she didn't know that I knew. The entire time I was around her, I knew something was off about the accusation. One thing led to another, and I was feeling some type of way about her," he confessed as we maneuvered the chest through the narrow doorframe.

"She's amazingly weird and intelligent," I piped with a light laughter before continuing, "Treat her right, man. That's all that I ask. That fuck nigga, Rondon, doesn't deserve her. He ain't good enough in my eyes."

Laughing, Juvy said, "I hate him. From day one, I didn't like his ass. He has it coming to him if he thinks he's going to have her... I'm claiming her and the baby."

Sighing heavily, I had to check myself before responding. I was a married man that lusted and wanted after the one woman that I couldn't have, all because of who was in our lives. After we were done fluffing and folding my father's body in the large, black and gold chest, we placed it in the back of my father's SUV.

I grabbed the gifts I bought her for Christmas and placed them in her tan and black hammock which was located on the right side of the nicely decorated porch. Afterwards, I told Juvy to hop in his Hummer and follow me. We left without so much as a word to X. On the way down the short, green pathway toward the gate, I saw her on the porch.

Twenty miles outside of the city limits of Clanton, I drove my father's truck into the deep pits of the woods and set it ablaze. Jumping in the Hummer with Juvy, we sat in the whip, smoked blunts, and chatted until the entire SUV was engulfed in flames. Leaving the wooded air, I told Juvy to drop me off at a service station.

"Mane, if need be, I can take you back to Montgomery," he told me as I hopped out.

"Nawl, we good. I'll have a way up outta here in an hour or so. Take care of her, man. If you need help in murking that fuck nigga, Rondon... shit... scroll through X's phone, and call me. I will surely help you in that deed! Tell her that I will always love her, no matter what, and that she won't have to worry about Taea being on her ass," I told him genuinely.

"I will do. Go home to your wife, and make things work. It was a reason why you asked her to marry you."

"Because she was the second best thing next to X," I informed him as I tapped on the windowsill before walking off.

When he tooted the horn and pulled away from the country, small service station, I was a mess... mentally. On the contrary, I knew I had to get my shit together, because I had children that I vowed I would never leave behind. I had a wife that I made vows to, and regardless of how I was feeling about X, I had to honor them. I was going to come clean about having sex with her and about my feelings toward her.

I was prepared for Taea to ask for a divorce. I was prepared to be a single man that co-parented with his ex-wife. I was prepared to not be able to see X another day in my life. I was prepared for another day of being a confused man.

Chapter Twelve

Taea

Sunday, December 31st

It had been five days since I'd placed my eyes on Bango, but I did talk to him. He called three times a day to check on the well-being of our children. A part of me wanted to know where he was, but then again, I didn't want my heart broken with the answers he was going to provide me.

I missed him terribly, but I wasn't going to let him know that. I was a mess, and I didn't know what to do. All I knew was that I wanted a loving life with a man that adored me and my babies. I wasn't for the games and coming second. I was tired of coming second.

"Taea," my grandmother called out from the living room.

"Yes, ma'am," I replied as I hopped off the bed and peeped my head around my door.

"Are you sure that you don't want Toot and I to help you off?" she inquired curiously.

"Yes, ma'am. I'm sure. It'll be a piece of cake once I return the car and board the airplane. They have people at the airport that are willing to help me," I informed her as I looked at my childhood bedroom for the final time.

"Okay."

"Goodbye, old room. It'll be a while before I come back down here," I voiced lightly to the room I grew up in.

Closing the door behind me, I held my head high as I strolled toward the living room where Grandma Toot, my kids, and my grandmother were. Surprised that Reggio and his other two children weren't sitting in the living room, I had to ask Grandma Toot if she'd seen either of them.

"No, baby, I haven't seen Reggio or those boys since the fiasco at Christmas," she replied as she fixed her glasses on the bridge of her nose.

"I wanted him to tell him goodbye. I guess I will call him before we board the plane."

"Have you talked to Bango today?" my grandmother asked sweetly as she ensured that MarTaea's straps were fastened tightly.

"He called this morning."

"What are y'all going to do?" she continued inquiring.

"I don't know, grandma," I told her honestly. She began talking about what she thought I should do, and I quickly looked at my watch. Seeing that my flight was due to leave out at 5:00 p.m., I wanted to leave out early just in case there was an accident on the highway.

Nipping my grandmother's ranting, I said softly, "Grandma, I gotta go. I don't want anything to delay us leaving this state."

"It's noon, Taea. You are good at running away from your problems. No wonder the man ain't returned down here to fix shit with you... you ran his ass away," she huffed.

"Now Sue, you know you dead ass wrong for that statement. You need to apologize, now!" Grandma Toot shouted as she shook her head.

"Nawl, Grandma Toot, she don't have to apologize," I stated angrily. I didn't know what possessed my grandmother to say that, but I'll let her have it.

Continuing, I said, "I guess you are the wife of the year, huh? You have a lot to say about my marriage and who I am as a woman... how *my* husband this and *my* husband that, but I don't see you with a man or a husband. What *my* husband and I do is our business. If I want to run, I can, because I'm a grown woman. Me running from my problems is no different than you running from yours! Now, have a nice day!"

Gathering my children's car seats, I fled to the rental car. Once inside, I made sure that their buckles were secured. Hopping in the front seat and starting the engine, I expected my grandmother to come out and apologize so that I could, but she didn't. Instead, Grandma Toot came out. We conversed for ten minutes before I told her that I would call the minute I touched down in Birmingham. As she passed out kisses, I was antsy to get the hell away from Montgomery, Alabama. I wasn't going to show my face for a long motherfucking time. Alabama wasn't my home anymore, and I was damn glad of that.

***

When my children and I arrived home, it was 8:45 p.m. If my children weren't completely drained, I knew for a fact that I was. Our luggage, their seats, and stroller tired me out, more so than changing their diapers and feeding them in the busy airports. I was very thankful that Gonzilla picked up the phone and was able to help me out. Soon after we laid the sleeping children down, I asked Gonzilla to stay over for a while so that we could play catch-up. Once she agreed, I ran to the kitchen, grabbed the most expensive bottle of wine, snatched two wine glasses of the wine glass rack, and plopped my ass on the comfortable sofa next to my nanny-turned-only-friend.

As I filled the wine glasses to the rim, I exhaled heavily before asking her how her holiday and family was.

"Girl, they are fine after the fiasco that took place prior to you leaving," she stated as she took a wine flute out of my hand.

"What happened?" I inquired nosily as I prayed that I wasn't the only one dealing with bullshit.

"My auntie found out that my father killed her dog freaking years ago, and she was holding him hostage in the kitchen with a knife," she stated with a serious face while shaking her head. Bursting out in laughter over the silliest shit I'd ever heard, it took Gonzilla to tell me to shut up before I stopped laughing. I had to know more about this story.

"Are you serious?" I inquired, still snickering.

"Yes, she had that dog for six years before my father killed it. Auntie was about ten when my grandfather bought her a French poodle. My father said that the dog kept chewing on his shoes, and he grew tired of the little thing shitting all over his room--on top of eating his shoes. One day, he decided to feed it bologna that was dipped in antifreeze."

Shaking my head and laughing at Gonzilla's story, I quickly stopped laughing as I realized that the auntie was hurt behind her brother killing something that she truly loved. I don't know if the glass of wine was getting to me, or the message of the story, but before I knew it, tears were streaming down my face. I began to sob uncontrollably as the wine glass tipped out of my hand.

"Oh, honey, what is wrong?" Gonzilla asked sincerely as she slid closer to me and placed me in the crook of her arms.

"I believe my marriage is over. Bango told me that he had the urge to sleep with the very woman that damn near killed him. The bitch had the nerve to show up at my grandmother's home, and he protected the woman from his father. He called her baby in front of my face... as if he forgot that he was married," I cried.

Gonzilla sat on my sofa and rocked me as I told her everything that happened between Bango and I, since we first slept together. As I relived the happy and sad moments of my life with him, I realized that I loved him more than I could ever express. On the contrary, I realized that I was a fool for him as well. There had been so many times that he pushed me; to the point that I thought I wouldn't be able to recover. Without a doubt, I believed this was one of those times that I was done turning away from the cliff--hopping back into his arms.

I was on the edge of the cliff, and I was ready to plunge head first into the river. I was at the point of no return. I was a fucking fool for love. I was willing to degrade myself, my way of thinking, and the very essence of being a strong, black woman for a man that gave two fucks about me and the way I felt for him. I was done being the fool; I was done giving him my all when all he was giving me was bullshit and lies. There was no way in hell I was going to continue my marriage with a man that thought it was okay to betray his marital vows for a woman that didn't mean him any good. I was too damn good for Bango, and it was time I started treating myself as the beautiful, intelligent Queen that I was.

Wiping the tears away from my face, I gave Gonzilla a half-smile and told her that I was alright.

"Honey, go and get you some rest. I will stay the night and aid you with the children. Don't you get up to check on them, because their godmother/nanny is here," she told me as she gave me a tight hug.

"Thank you," I stated softly as I slowly lifted off the sofa.

"If you want to vent more to get your answers, you know I am ten steps away from you."

"I know," I replied before leaving the living room. Before making a sharp right turn into the hallway, I swiftly turned around and said genuinely, "Zilla, thank you for everything you have done for me and my babies."

"No, Taea, thank you," she replied sweetly as she wiped a tear away from her eye.

Blowing kisses at her before I sped down the hallway, the house phone began to ring. Quickly walking into my room, I snatched the black cordless phone off the cradle. Staring at my husband's cell phone number, my hand trembled as I pressed the talk button.

"Hello," I breathed softly into the phone.

"Hey. How are you and the kids?" he asked in a tone that indicated that he'd been crying.

"They are fine," I replied blankly.

"That's good, but you didn't answer my question… how are you doing?"

"As good as I'm going to get."

"We need to talk."

"I'm not up for talking tonight, Bango. I'm tired. The flight drained me completely," I informed him as I walked into the master bedroom, aiming for the garden tub.

"I'll be back home tomorrow. I'm home for good. No more trips or *missions*."

Ignoring the fact that he said home, I rapidly dropped a question on him as I turned the water knobs inside of the tub.

"What you want to talk about? I gotta make sure that I have my mental right," I stated nastily as I stripped out of my clothing.

"X... us, our future, etc."

"I can sum all of that shit up for you... tomorrow, I am seeking a lawyer, and I will be filing for divorce. You don't have to explain shit to me. We weren't meant for each other, Bango... well... not in the sense of being married to one another."

"Taea, shut up. I need my best friend now."

That shit really pissed me the fuck off, and I was going to let him know why.

"Why every time you get in some shit, and it hurts me deeply, you need your fucking best friend? I'm tired of being your best friend when you fuck up! Why can't I be that same damn best friend while I'm your wife? Why should I separate the title best friend and wife, Bango? Why should I hear all the shit that's going to kill the wife title, huh?"

"Because, it'll make us better, Taea. I should've been told you how I felt. I should've told you about X, and I'm sorry. I didn't. I put on a façade for so long that I started to believe the shit. I fucked up, and I'm truly sorry. If you want to divorce me, that is fine, because I deserve to be by myself. I deserve everything that's going to come to me. I want a clean slate with you… even if we aren't together. I want to see you happy, and if it's not with me, then with someone else. I don't want you angry with me anymore. I don't want to hold anything in from you. We have to be on cordial terms for the sake of our children. Believe it or not, a nigga love you."

Oh, that word *love* was overused, and I lost it. As I told my husband a thing or two about love, he was completely quiet. By the time I was done with my speech, Bango was crying, and I knew he was hurt. That was my first time in a long time that I'd heard him cry.

Calming down and focusing on why he was crying, I asked curiously, "Why are you crying, Bango? What is really going on?"

"I'm tired of lying. I'm tired of hurting you. I'm tired of seeing you cry... all because I'm the confused one. Taea, go file for divorce, and I will sign the papers, because you deserve better. I'll be by tomorrow to grab my things and to do my fatherly duties with our children. I'll call you when I land," he voiced softly.

Silence overcame the phone, and I surely didn't know what to think. As I turned the water off and added bath beads to the tub, I slipped my aching feet into the mostly hot water, followed by submerging my body in the soothing water. Mind on one million, my heart began to sink. Why, when I did nothing wrong... I couldn't begin to tell myself.

"Well, I'll talk to you tomorrow. Goodnight, and kiss our babies for me," he voiced sadly. I wanted to tell him that I didn't want to end the call, but my tongue wasn't cooperating with me.

Therefore, I voiced casually, "Okay and goodnight."

Neither one of us hung up the phone. We just cried on the phone together. Deep down, I knew that Bango had some shit to tell me by his behavior. A part of me wanted to know what he had to say, and another part of me didn't.

Curiosity got the best of me, so my crazy ass asked, "What is really going on, Bango?"

"I still love X. The feelings never went away. I thought they did, but I was just masking them by wanting to kill her... thinking that she was out to get me. Once I was in her presence, I knew that she was innocent in harming me. I knew that she was looking out for me, and keeping me close, because she still had feelings for me. I'd recently slept with her. I became angry once she told me that she was pregnant with another man's child. I felt hurt that she would allow someone to get her pregnant. I was ready to murder the nigga that she was pregnant by. Her uncle and my dad ruined what she and I could've had. I was fucking angry at them for how she turned out. They fucking destroyed her very being and got her tied into some shit that she had no business in. They turned an innocent, sweet person into a vicious killing machine that's scared of love... the same love that was introduced into her life by me!"

Hearing my best friend turned husband say those things about another woman had me in tears. I didn't know how to interpret any of those things. I couldn't produce any questions. I couldn't curse him out, and I couldn't breathe. I felt as if I was dreaming. I pinched myself to wake up from the horrible dream, as my husband jumped on why he fell into my arms.

"Truth be told, you were my rebound female. You were the one that took my mind off X and our love life. You were a breath of fresh ai—"

I hung the phone up in his face, and I'll be damned if he didn't call back. I clicked the talk button and then hung it up again. I counted to three and pressed the talk button. Pleased that I heard a dial tone, I left the phone on so that he wouldn't be calling the house phone all night.

There was no way in hell I was going to allow him to throw me a boomerang. There was no way I was going to fall into the trap that he was throwing at me. I wasn't going for the shit he was trying to serve me, so that I wouldn't file for divorce. He thought that he was going to butter me up after telling me that he slept with a bitch that he loved... a bitch that had caused my life pure hell. Oh, fuck no! I wasn't going to be his rebound bitch anymore!

Chapter Thirteen

Rondon

Checking my voicemail, I had several nasty messages from X, stating that my mother called her phone on Christmas talking crazy. With a puzzled look upon my face, I quickly dialed my mother's cell phone to see what her problem was. On the third ring, she answered the phone, and I began with my interrogation.

"What gives you the right to call X's phone, Ma? How in the hell did you get her number in the first place?" I asked in an upset tone while sitting upright on my large bed, staring at my beige wall.

"Because I am your mother, and I can do anything that I please. Don't worry about how I got her number. Reginald, that bitch is causing you to lose your entire mind. Not one holiday God has blessed us with, you haven't been present. Does the bitch have you voodooed or some shit?"

"Ma, you sound like a mad woman. Hell nawl, I don't have any roots put on me. I chose not to visit y'all, because I simply don't want to be bothered with you. Regardless of how you feel about X... that still didn't give you the right to call her phone. The only way you got her number was through my phone. Stop going through my phone, looking for shit to start... especially, with someone that's never done anything to you," I told her as I balled and opened my fists. I really wanted to hop on a plane and face the woman.

"I can do whatever the fuck I please, because you are my son... a son that acts like he can't obey my rules and regulations," she retorted.

"This is why we can't get along. You continue to meddle in my business. Do I meddle in yours? Have I ever? Even when you continuously cheated on dad with Roger's wife's father?" I voiced casually before sniggering.

The gasp that left my mother's mouth informed me that she was shocked that I voiced her wrong doings, or either she was shocked that I knew, so I continued on.

"If you want to keep on meddling in my life, I will destroy yours. How would father like to know that his loving wife is screwing the man that comes over on holidays with his daughter... or that you fucked him prior to y'all coming down to Miami for Flema's funeral... or that he accompanies you on "business trips", or the simple fact that you have been drinking a lot of herbal tea with parsley leaves in it, buying ginger root, and house tons of blue and black cohosh pills?"

I laughed at the woman that swore she knew it all. For a while, there was silence on my mother's end to the point I had to say, "Hello?"

"I'm here, Reginald," my mother stated in a low tone. I could tell that she was clenching her teeth.

"Do you have anything to say? Am I making speculations? You know I can provide proof of the allegations I am making. One thing the mother of my child taught me was to gather evidence, and I made sure to get plenty of it," I snickered sarcastically.

"Do not say a word to your father about the things you are speaking on, understood?" she announced in a passive voice.

"You are going to respect my child's mother, understood? You are going to give her the chance to warm your heart like she's done mine, understood? You say one thing wrong about her, and I will personally give dad the videos and papers on your little lingering love affair, understood? You have a great day, mother," I proudly stated before I hung up the phone.

Lying back on the bed, I had a huge grin on my face as I finally had my mother clutching her pearls. I would've loved to be a fly on the wall right now at her and dad's house. I would call around the time I thought he would be home from one of his golf games, to check on Mother Dearest.

As I was thanking myself for setting up videos throughout my parents' home and her workplace, my cell phone sounded off. Looking at the screen, I sighed heavily as Jacquel's name displayed across my screen.

Answering the phone roughly, I spat, "What, guh?"

"I miss you. I want us to work things out. When are you going to come over?" she whined.

"Mane, what is wrong with you? You don't have any respect about yourself. You let me dog you out and treat your home any kind of way. Why in the hell do you want a nigga like me in your presence, when I clearly show that I have no interest in you?" I inquired curiously.

I had to see what was going on in her head. For years, I wondered why she let me do her the way I did. Jacquel wasn't a bad looking female at all—average.

"Rondon, I've had my eyes on you since we attended Alabama State University years ago. I've always liked you. You were never the guy you are pretending to be now. You had manners. I know that this façade you are putting on is for that broad you be underneath. You were not a street nigga. You were a damn nerd."

Laughing and agreeing with her, I replied, "You are correct. I wasn't a street nigga, and I'm still a nerd… just in a street nigga's attire and demeanor. I've learned so much by being a street nigga. I know you project, wanna-be-classy, weave-patting, outfit-swapping, passenger-seat-riding, hot-Cheetos-and-pickle-eating, fuck-your-boys-in-one-setting, leggings-wearing, letting-a-nigga-trap-out-yo'-house hoes love street niggas, and y'all will do anything to get pregnant and wife'd up by one. So, with that being said, I know your mother didn't raise you to be one of those types of hoes. Jacquel, go to another city where a nigga don't know you and settle down with a regular Joe. This dick here belongs to the chick I be underneath. I been tired of slinging this grade A dick into a grade F pussy. Good night, bitch!"

Crying softly in the phone, she spoke.

"Why are you so ruthless and such a savage?"

"The streets made me a savage, bitch. You are dismissed. You call my phone again, mention me on social media, or speak to me in the public, I will have you no longer breathing. You think I'm playing... bitch, try me," I voiced sternly before hanging up the phone.

Throwing my phone on the bed, I began to think about the one woman I turned a savage for. Quickly picking up the phone, I dialed X's number. Immediately, her voicemail picked up. Growing angry at her not answering any of my calls, texts, or emails, I slammed my phone on the soft covers of my bed.

"I swear, woman, when I find you... I'mma hold your ass hostage. You gon' talk to me, and you are going to hear me out," I voiced aloud, dropping my head against the bed.

Zapp and Roger's song "I Want To Be Your Man" played on 97.1, and I fell in sync with song. As I sang, I was thinking of ways that I could prove to X that I really wanted to be in her life. I had to show her that no one could love her like I could. She had to know the true feelings I possessed for her.

Never in a million years would I want her to feel that being with me was a waste of time. I wanted to show her that I would never make her feel like her uncle did. I was a completely different breed of a man than her uncle; I was a real man that knew how to treat and please his woman. I was willing to do anything to show her that I was the best male to be in her life. Quickly grabbing my phone, I called the one person that I tried to avoid talking to...Ruger. If anyone knew X, it would be him. On the third ring, he answered.

"Aye, Ruger... I need you. I don't want anyone with X but me. I need my girl back. What do I need to do to make her see that I love her?"

"Give her space. She'll come around," he announced blankly.

"Ruger, that is not enough," I spat.

"I'm telling you what you need to do. Either you take the advice or not. One thing about that stubborn woman is that she likes her space so that she can think, critically. We all treated her like Tyke did, and right now, she is trying to find herself."

Intrigued by him agreeing that we treated her like Tyke, I wanted to know more.

"How did we treat her like Tyke?"

"I'll be over there as soon as I get through doing what I'm doing."

With a quizzical look upon my face, I was going to ask him what he was doing, but I quickly thought against it.

"Aight."

Killing time until Ruger showed his face, I hopped on social media and laughed my behind off at the stupid memes and videos that were posted. Scrolling down my timeline, I saw an interesting post that had me smiling hard. Throwing down my phone, I ran to the shower, cut it on, and quickly found clothing to put on. Before I hopped in the shower, I sent out a text to Baked and J-Money to get their asses to my house immediately. As soon as they replied okay, off to the shower I went.

"Ooouuu!" I shouted as I skipped toward the steamy bathroom.

Chapter Fourteen

Juvy

I'd been in Miami for three days, and I was ready to get back to my X. Being in the city was depressing and downright frustrating. The atmosphere and memories were extremely toxic to me. All I could think about was my days of ripping and running the streets with my supposed to be brothers and dealing with Flema and her attitude. Throughout my time of being in Miami, I found myself laughing briefly followed by throwing things around my little spot.

I had two tasks to complete while I was down here... kill the Jocktons, and make things right with my children. Since killing them was number one priority, I had to make sure I knew where they were before striking them. I couldn't let them get away with what they had done to my family or me. The way they befriended me was despicable, and I didn't like it one bit. All this mess goes back to Reggio, and I was glad that nigga was dead. Honestly, I wanted to blow his head off.

When Bango clipped his father, I was amazed, but a part of me felt Bango's pain as he unloaded his entire clip in the man's dome. The look on X's face when Bango killed Reggio... the hurt and frustration was in her face as well. I really believed that she wanted to do it so that Bango wouldn't have to live with that agony.

After thinking of that crazy, confused guy made me wonder how he was doing, what he was doing, and whether he was okay. I hoped he was able to get his mind right and make an attempt to reconcile things with his wife. He was tormented from the past events that took place with his father and X's uncle. There was an undeniable love between them, and I had to respect that. They had been to hell and back, all because of how they felt for each other and their positions in the streets. I couldn't tell either of them not to love one another. Who was I to demand that? Their love for the other had a hand in how they viewed and respected love. On the contrary, I could demand that X not have sex with him, especially if she wanted to be involved with me.

Seeing how she looked at me versus how she looked at him, I didn't have to demand it. She had it instilled in her mind. When she pulled out her shotgun, I knew she did it so that she could get some act right out of us. She didn't show favoritism toward us. When she spoke roughly to Bango, I got the same treatment.

Ring. Ring. Ring.

Pulling my thoughts away from the crazy scene that took place days ago, I grabbed my phone from the light blue holster and answered Tania's call.

"Hello," my deep, baritone voice stated soothingly as I slowed my Hummer for a yellow light on the main street of downtown Miami.

"I missed your call. What's up?" she asked at the same time she closed a door.

"I want to formally meet my children as their father. However, I don't want Bone and Fish to know about it. Where are those idiots?" I quickly rushed into the phone as I noticed the traffic light turning green.

"Bone and Fish are in the game room. They have the door closed… which you already know what that means. I'm not sure how long they'll be here," she replied quickly in a low tone.

Something wasn't right; I could tell by the volume of her voice. There had to been an uproar at their home. Her voice spoke levels without directly telling me.

"Okay... umm, I'll tell you what... take the kids to Alice Wainwright Park. Make enough food for a picnic," I told her sternly as I headed toward the beautifully preserved nature park.

"Okay," she replied again in the same tone. I had to know what was up; therefore, I asked.

"Tania?" I inquired.

"Yes?"

"Is everything okay?"

"No," she stated with a semi-shaken timbre.

"What's wrong?"

"Fish is out to get you, and he doesn't mind letting everyone know. I don't understand what in the hell is going on and why. He's making Bryson and Taylor's lives hell right now for no reason. I tried to step in and protect them, but he put his hands on me. It took Bone to get him away from us and the children. While they are in the room, I've taken some of the children's clothes and put them in the van. I can't have any of the children around his rage."

Immediately, I felt awkward by the mentioning of Fish mistreating my kids. True enough, I did the same thing to them by disowning them. However, they were innocent beings and shouldn't be subjected to any harm. Quickly placing myself back into my ten-year-old mind frame and then returned back to my grown man adult mind set, I felt ashamed for how I treated them, and I was angry at myself and Fish for our behavior toward them.

"What exactly is he doing to them?"

"Telling them nasty things such as we aren't their real parents, and their real parents don't love or want them. Taylor has been crying since Fish returned an hour ago. What is going on between the two of y'all?" she questioned as opened a door.

"I'll explain everything once you get to the park. I'm ten minutes away. Don't even worry about fixing food. I'll take y'all out to eat. Get to the park as soon as possible."

"Okay," she breathed before hanging up the phone.

Once Tania was off the phone, my thoughts began on how I was going to pull everything off. Pulling into the park, I stepped out of my vehicle and fired up a cigarette. Standing beside my Hummer, I lifted my head toward the sky, and allowed the bright sun to beat down on my black face. Closing my eyes, flashes of X's smiling face appeared which caused me to smile.

With my cell phone in my hand, I pressed and held down on the number two button. Seconds later, the line began to ring. On the third ring, the beautiful voice sang hello.

The smile on my face was brighter than the sun. The happiness in my heart was that of a child going to Disney World for the first time.

"Hey, beautiful Mrs. Bossy. How is your day?"

"It's going good so far. These heifers getting on my nerves," she stated in an agitated tone as I heard loud women in the back.

Chuckling, I replied, "I see that you hate being around females. Give them a chance, X. You are stepping into a new life, and you gotta have a smooth transition from being around a bunch of males into a loud pack of women."

"I'm trying, but I'm not used to bitches cackling and shit. I'm use to dominoes being slammed on the table by a bunch of shit talking men. That's all that I know," she whined.

Chuckling heavily, I responded, "I know. It'll get easier as the days go by. Are you at least enjoying the beautiful day?"

"Yes, I am. I wish you were here."

With a smile that hadn't left my face, I replied happily, "Me too. Hopefully, I'll be touching back in Alabama before the end of the night."

"I hope so. I'm missing my Mr. Bossy," she cooed into the phone.

"Mr. Bossy missing his Mrs. Bossy."

"Awww. How's the visit going?"

"Today is my first day seeing them. I had to check out some things first," I told her, without going into too much detail.

"Okay. Well you make sure that you spend as much time with them as you can."

"I will. X, what am I supposed to do with them?" I inquired curiously as I looked around the park, hoping that Tania would be slinging her gray van in soon.

Laughing lightly, X responded casually, "Talk to them. Get to know them better. Take them out to eat, to the park, or something of that nature."

"No... not activities... but as far as raising them."

"Oh that... I'm sorry. What do you feel like doing?"

"I don't know what I want to do. I know I gotta make things right with them. They didn't ask to be here, so I gotta man up like you said and handle my business."

"Do you want to co-parent with their mother?"

"Hell no."

"I believe the question you are trying to ask me is will I help raise them with you?" she voiced softly. Without answering immediately, I believe that was what I was truly hinting at.

"Ummm," she voiced strongly, trying to get me to answer.

"I think that's what I'm hinting at," I replied, fumbling with my brown collared shirt.

"Nawl, I don't need you to think, baby. I need you to know," she announced in a bossy tone.

"Yes, ma'am," I responded quickly and then continued, "X, if I decided to bring my children to Alabama with me, will you help me raise them?"

"Yes, I will."

With a smile on my face, I said excitedly, "Cool."

We chatted until I saw Tania's van pull beside my vehicle. Hanging up the phone with X, I became nervous as I placed my eyes on the two children that I made with Wilema. Bryson and Taylor were a beautiful shade of bronze with a body build that resembled mine. Bryson hopped out of the van and was smiling as he ran to me. Holding out my arms, I kept my eyes on Taylor as she stood to the side of the van with her eyes planted on the ground. Tania's other children spoke to me briefly before running off into the gorgeous green land of the park.

"What's up, man?" I asked Bryson as I picked him up.

"Coolin'," he voiced happily as I burst out laughing.

"Taylor... what's wrong, baby girl?" I inquired curiously as if I didn't know.

"Nothing," she lied as she continued looking at the ground.

"May I get a hug, please?"

"Sure," she replied as she looked at Tania who nodded her head.

Slowly walking toward me, I saw Flema all over again, and I damn near shed a tear. My daughter resembled her aunt which brought a terrible feeling abroad. I had to shake the feeling out of me before it destroyed what I was trying to do.

Soon as Taylor made it to me, I hugged her tightly and told her that everything was going to be alright. Her response almost knocked the breath out of me.

"No it won't, Uncle Juvy. My brother and I aren't wanted by our real parents, so how is everything going to be alright?"

That statement alone let me know that I had to set things right, but I had to be careful on the delivery of my information. So, I looked at Tania and asked casually, "Are you ready to help me?"

"I've been waiting on this day for a long time."

She smiled as she began to walk toward us.

"Bryson and Taylor, I am your father. There are some things that took place that kept me away from y'all as your father. The details aren't important to know right now. I'm here to make things right with y'all. One thing you guys don't have to worry about is me not being in your life and not raising you. I'm not going anywhere," I began to say as I put Bryson down and motioned for us to stroll along.

***

It was 9:30 p.m. when I left the hotel where I was staying. I was feeling great after the conversation I'd had earlier with my children and Tania. Tania and I came up with a plan that would allow me to see them, until I had a for sure plan for taking them. Her fear was how they would adapt without her, since she was all that they knew. Plus, Taylor agreed that they wanted to live with Tania until they were comfortable with me. Bryson liked the idea of for living with me. Tania's main concern was how Fish was going to continue bullying the children, and I quickly told her don't worry about that.

After the kids went to enjoy each other's company, I quickly briefed her on the happenings of what Bone, Fish, and their mother had been up to. Immediately, she knew that I couldn't let them breathe a moment longer.

"How may I help you, sir?" a chubby, bright-skinned nurse asked me with a smile upon her long, shaped face.

"I'm here to see Nurse Wilema Willington," I told her casually.

"Okay. I will page her," she voiced happily before paging Wilema.

Strolling away from the information desk on the fourth floor of Wilema's workplace, I began to whistle to myself. Not knowing how this conversation would go, I prayed for the best outcome. I was willing to undo the mess that I created ten years ago. I was willing for Wilema to be a mother to our children. However, I was going to inform her that I wasn't going to put up with any bullshit.

Five minutes later, Wilema ambled toward me with a pleasant yet surprised look on her face as she toyed with the McDonald's cup that sat in her hand.

"What do I owe the pleasure of having you showing up at my workplace, Juvy?"

"I would like for us to talk about Bryson and Taylor. Are you available to give me twenty-five minutes of your time?" I asked cordially while glaring into her eyes.

"Sure. We can walk outside," she informed me before walking to the nurse's station and briefly talking to the chubby woman. Three minutes later, we were outside in the light breezy night, discussing the children that we made together.

The conversation went well, until Wilema stated, "We are going to be one happy family."

Looking at the broad with a quizzical facial expression, I had to hurry up and rectify her statement.

"No ma'am, Wilema. That is not what I'm implying. What I'm saying is that we will co-parent our children. *You* and *I* will not be in a relationship together. I just want our kids to know and love their parents. That's it. There has never or will ever be anything going on between the two of us."

Smacking her lips, she replied curtly, "If we are going to co-parent, we will be together. That's the only way it's going to work. Do you understand that I love you? I want to be with you. I went through hell and back just to get pregnant the second time by you."

With a frown upon my face, I had to know how far she went to get pregnant by me the second time.

"Explain," I mumbled lowly as two people appeared with cigarettes in their mouths.

Chuckling lightly, she responded, "Honey, I drugged you. You weren't willing to give up the dick without a condom on. Once the drug took its place, it was a piece of cake, getting you to fuck me repeatedly without a condom on. Even though you called me Flema countless times... I didn't mind as long as I was getting what I wanted... another swollen belly... another one of Juvian's babies."

Not able to respond to the bitch, I just glared at her.

"Don't look at me like that. I wanted what my sister had. Thus, I got it by any means necessary. I loved every minute of what I did to you and what you did to me, granted you thought that I was Flema."

Right then, something in my head confirmed that she had motive for Flema being out of the way. How I was going to prove it was a great question.

Kicking me out of my thoughts, Wilema stated aggressively, "So, what are we going to do, Juvy?"

"I'm raising my kids with or without you. I'm not going to be forced in a relationship with a woman I didn't love and will never love."

"Did you love my sister?" she asked and laughed.

"Something like that."

"Not how you was digging in this pussy the first time. You couldn't have had an ounce of love for her," she retorted as she waltzed closer to me.

Rolling my eyes, I grew agitated with the bitch. She was bold, and I was dumb for thinking that we could be cordial with one another on that parenting tip. I had one more thing to accomplish, and I was ready for this conversation to be over with.

Therefore, I told her sternly, "You have one day to think this through before I go with my final decision of casting you out of their lives."

Huffing as she placed her hands around my neck, she softly stated, "Don't make me gather information against you. I know some pretty powerful people that will be willing to get their hands on the biggest drug dealer in Miami. I'm very sure they would be anxious to know who was setting people's businesses and homes on fire, and I'm damn sure they would like to know who blew up Marco's mother's home... you did murder them, remember?"

Clenching and unclenching my jaw, I placed my hands into the front pockets of my jeans, looked into the calm starry sky, and sighed heavily... all the while hearing Wilema's rants.

"I refused to come second to a bitch that couldn't offer you shit," she whispered against my neck.

"What?" I asked curiously as I brought my face close to hers. At the same time, I unscrewed a vial that was hidden in my pocket.

"I said, I refused to come second to a bitch that couldn't offer you shit. What could Flema give you that I couldn't? What could she bring to the table other than a pussy, mouth, and an asshole?"

I had to keep her talking so that I could quickly slide the contents into her mouth, but those two smokers were outside chatting away. Time was of the essence, and I was praying heavily that they left soon.

"Oh, so you can't answer me?" Wilema piped as she rubbed my face. I wanted to pull away, but I didn't want to raise any alarm, especially since I was planning on murdering this bitch on the hospital's grounds.

"There was nothing that she could offer me, Wilema," I stated casually as I brought my mouth to hers.

I gave that bitch the best kiss of her life. As I heard the smokers leaving the area, I had my eyes sealed on them until they disappeared around the corner. I brought my hand out of my pockets and held on to the vial. I had to pick the right time to remove my mouth from hers. When I felt the moment was right, I removed my mouth at the same time I gripped her jaws tightly. Once my mission was complete, I shoved the contents in the black vial down her mouth. Oh, she tried to put up a fight, but I wouldn't allow her to.

Dropping the vial on the ground at the same time I snatched Wilema's body close to mine, I smiled sweetly in her face. She began to yell, but I pinched her backside to the point she started crying.

"Shut the fuck up, Wilema. You will not be breathing any longer. My new girlfriend taught me how to make a poisonous concoction. I will see you in hell when I get there, or even if I go there," I laughed before seeing her eyes dart rapidly.

"Why... are... you... such... a ... savage...?" she voiced in between breathing.

"Because the fucking streets made me one," I whispered in her ear with a smile on my face.

Her body began to grow limp, and the performance from me came about immediately. Pretending to be distraught, I bent down and picked up the vial and shoved it in my pocket. Yelling help as I ran with Wilema in my arms toward the entrance door, a ninja was happy that she was dying in my arms. I knew for a fact that there would be no hope for her.

It seemed like forever before a gurney was brought forth and an outstretched Wilema was laid out on it. They rushed her inside and began doing their job.

In the emergency room, I waited patiently for them to report that she was dead. At 10:30 p.m., I got my answer when the attending doctor calmly told me that Wilema was no longer breathing. I didn't cry, but I surely acted like I felt bad for the woman. The man asked me did I need any counseling, and I told him that I didn't. The next question came about which was, did I want to see her for a final time, and of course, I replied with a yes.

Two minutes later, I was staring at a cold Wilema. On the inside, I was smiling, but on the outside, no one would've known.

I bent toward her ear and said nastily, "What goes around comes around, bitch. You killed your sister, thinking that you could have me. Sorry, bitch, another angel stole and took my heart. She even stole it right from underneath your sister." Planting a kiss on her ear, I left the room. Outside of the hospital, I rushed to my Hummer, because I still had one thing that must be taken care of. I was going to sit back and wait for the fire trucks to wail.

Driving rapidly to The Warehouse, I placed a call to Tania to check on her and the kids. She informed me that they were at my spot. Confirmation gave me the go ahead to call Ms. Jockton's house phone. I was praying that Bone or Fish answered the phone.

On the third ring of Fish answering the phone, I heard laughter from Ms. Jockton and Bone while music was playing in the background.

"Goodbye, so called brother... if I make it to hell, I will see y'all there," I stated sternly before pulling out the homemade cell phone detonator and pressing the call button on it.

The line went dead before he could respond. Sitting at The Warehouse, I heard the explosion. While I was at the park with the children, I had Tania drop off two duffel bags filled with Bone's and Fish's clothing. She had no idea that in the bottom of the bag sat six bombs. X helped me make them, and she set them to the detonator that I held dearly in my hand.

Placing the gearshift in drive, I rammed my whip into one of the back doors of The Warehouse. Hopping out with the cell phone detonator and three bombs, I armed the explosives in the trunk of the hummer before busting out the small glass in the dented door. Arming the bombs, I chucked them inside of my old workplace and quickly ran to my charcoal Ferrari that was located a short distance from The Warehouse. As I hopped inside, I quickly put the key in the ignition and peeled away. Two blocks away from The Warehouse, I mashed the green button on the cell phone and the firework show began--again.

Oh, the smile on my face was glorious and beautiful as I saw the fire show take place. As I hopped on the main street of downtown Miami, I couldn't wait to be in X's arms. I couldn't wait to begin a new life with her and my children. As I came to a halt for a yellow light, sirens were going crazy, and I had to make sure that my deeds were done. Heading toward the once Jockton's home, I grew antsy as I neared their street.

Not able to turn on the street, I was amazed at the amount of firepower X had set me up with. Those damn devices took out six homes. I had to pray for the souls that I took, if they were home... minus the Jocktons. Rolling down my window, I asked the uniformed officers what took place.

"A house blew up, causing five other homes to crumble," the officer stated in a shocked tone before shaking his head.

Before I could say anything, I heard an elderly woman yell, "I'm so glad we weren't home, or we would've been dead."

"Any injuries or casualties?" I asked the officer.

"We aren't sure yet, sir."

Nodding my head, I put my whip in park and sat there to watch the firefighters do their job. As I waited in my car, I fired up a Cuban cigar and smoked that motherfucker. I wasn't leaving until I saw with my own eyes that the Jockton's were being carried out in a body bag.

An hour later, the street went crazy as the news of three bodies were recovered from the Jockton's home, three more deceased bodies were found in another home, and six more people were being transported to the hospital for injuries. As I learned of the news, I prayed for those three that died and for the six injured people.

Satisfied with the Jockton's fate, I slowly peeled away from the street and aimed for the Interstate. I was ready to be in the arms of my woman.

"Until next time, Miami. Have a fucking good one!" I shouted out the window as I sped out of the hellhole.

Chapter Fifteen
X

It was a gorgeous sunny, lightly breezy Saturday in Gulf Shores, Alabama. The atmosphere was great, and the vibes were enticing. I wished that Juvy was with me. The day would've been perfect with him close to me. However, he had business that sought his attention. He was taking care of more important business in Miami... mending things with his children.

As I was standing on the balcony of the condo I owned, eating a light lunch and enjoying the scenery, my cousin Keithia and her little entourage slid through the balcony's door. My cousins little crew spoke, and I threw up my hand. Those bitches were loud mouthed leeches, but they knew how to have fun. On the contrary, I hated being around my cousin's friends. It was Juvy's idea for me to invite them along. What he didn't know was that I was planning on ducking my cousin and her friends.

The sole reason of agreeing to get away from my normal territory was to visit Club Vela's owner, Mano. I had to pick up some money from him, even though he was good about running up to The Gump to deliver my coins. I told him that I would come down since Juvy made the suggestion for me to get out. Plus, I really needed the break from the past day's events.

Club Vela was a beach club that housed the street niggas and the groupies that came with the street life. This weekend was a damn good choice, because everyone and their mothers were out in Gulf Shores, enjoying their family and friends. The positive attitude and smiling faces of those visiting the city brought about a great feeling inside of me.

"What are you doing tonight, X?" Pea asked excitedly as she clinked her long nails together.

Pea was two years older than me with two children, and neither one of them had any manners. As I scanned over her petite body, I prayed heavily that she wouldn't draw too much attention to me tonight with her ghetto fabulous attitude.

"Not sure, yet. Let's link up," I responded while scrunching my face. I was quickly regretting my suggestion once I heard the other two chicken heads chirping and clapping.

"I can't believe you asked us to tag along. Can y'all, Keithia, Tay, Bri, and Meka?" Pea inquired in a high-pitched tone as she held a devilish smile.

"Hell nawl, guh. You know X has a certain type of taste that she likes with her?" Meka stated while looking at her long, colorful fake nails.

"I'm honored to hang out with you, X," Tay and Bri sang in unison before plastering a Kool-Aid smile across their chunky faces.

I shook my head, because I knew it was going to be one hell of a night with those broads. I'd known all of the chicks for years. Hell, all of us went to school together, and nothing had changed about them.

Tay and Bri were some ugly ass identical twins, no lie! Those black women had a forehead out of this world, jacked up teeth, big bell pepper noses, short and chunky in all the wrong places, and chronic acne. To top things off, they had the nerve to have four golds on their bottom teeth. The twins had perfectly rounded, light brown eyes and perfectly arched eyebrows with naturally long, curled eyelashes.

Meka was the complete opposite of the twins. She was very pretty. She was tall and athletic with flawless tanned skin that white women wished they had without paying a tanning salon. Her naturally long, curled black eyelashes and black curly hair led me to believe that she was mixed with Black and Puerto Rican.

"Bih, you serious, aren't you?" Keithia inquired as she stared at me. She was shocked as hell, and the look on her face caused me to laugh.

"Yes, I am," I responded with a smile and the shaking of my head.

"'Bout time you did decide to hang out with the one cousin that truly knows how to have fun, skee," Keithia chuckled, holding up her hands so that her little crew could give her a high five.

"Every time I see Rondon, he's forever asking me have I seen or talked to you," my cousin voiced as she took a seat in the white lounge chair. I exhaled heavily, and that cow continued to talk.

"You still haven't talked to him, have you?" she probed as I ignored her nosy tail by tucking my earbuds into my ears.

I didn't want to think about that asshole. I left him a swell message for giving his funky ass mother my number. She was another reason I had to get away. I was ready to put a hole in her head while her son watched!

With the music blasting in my ears, I ran my mind through my bedroom's closet and dressers for a lovely, comfortable outfit for the night's event. In my mind, I vividly saw the six different outfits that I would be eye candy in. My nails, toes, eyebrows, and eyelashes were done, so I didn't have to worry about any of those things. My hair was freshly braided, so I was good in the hair department.

As I thought about what I was going to wear, Michel'le's song "Something in My Heart" played on my phone. I quickly answered with a smile on my face. It was Mr. Bossy. As we talked, I rubbed the bottom of my uncomfortable abdomen. Once we were off the phone, my lined rang, and I ignored the calls from Rondon and Ruger.

I didn't see a need for answering their calls. They got what they wanted. Soon after, I received a call that I was patiently waiting on.

"Talk to me," I ushered in the phone.

"Two down and eleven more to go," the deep voiced stated quickly.

"Take care of all of them. I'll be tuned into WSFA," I replied casually before hanging up the phone with a beautiful smile on my face.

***

I decided to wear a red, crop top shirt that crisscrossed in the back and denim, high-rise skinny jeans. The stiletto heels and accessories color was red. A red studded nose ring was tucked into my left nostril, while a set of red balls were tightened on the ends of the red barbell. I decided that I didn't want to wear my prescription glasses, so I put in my all-red prescription contacts. At 10:00 p.m., I did a final check of my appearance and noticed I didn't have my gold bottom grill in. I walked into the bathroom, opened the container that housed my grill, and placed it perfectly on my bottom teeth. I smiled and flexed in the mirror.

"Yasss, you a bad mamma jamma tonight, Ms. Toole," I stated loudly to myself. Pleased with my appearance, I walked to the sitting area where Keithia and her entourage were.

"Oooh, shit now. She showing all the way out tonight. No black... well damn," Bri said in between inhales of the cigarette she held to her lips.

"I'm plain Jane tonight," I said and laughed lightly.

"That ass ain't plain Jane," Tay shouted. Everyone laughed, including me. I walked over to the fridge and reached on top of it to retrieve my keys. Once I had them in my hands, I dangled them while walking to the door. That was my way of telling them it was time to go.

"Come on here, heifers. It's party time," Pea demanded, walking out the door.

Ten minutes of fighting with the stairs, and we finally reached my 2014 black on black Range Rover. As soon as I fired up the engine, my speakers began to knock. People were out in the lightly breezy, supposed to be, winter's air; it was time to do a little shining and stunting. Before heading to Club Vela, I pulled into the nearest service station to fill up my truck, purchase some mints, and a bottle of water.

"It's going to be some fun in the city tonight, ladies!" Pea shouted after I turned down the radio.

"It surely is," Meka replied while I slowly strolled toward pump ten.

I turned off the engine and dug around in the console to get my wallet. When I found it, I turned around to see Rondon walking into the store. My heart pumped faster, and I started panting.

I started chanting to myself, *Don't start no shit, Rondon! Don't start no shit, Rondon!*

"Which one of you motherfuckers put something on social media?" I asked sternly as I looked in each of their faces.

No one said a thing, so I asked the question again as I pulled my nine from under the seat.

"Okay, okay. It was me," Meka confessed. I looked at her and rolled my eyes as hard as I could.

"X, put the gun up... please. She didn't mean to. I forgot to tell her not to post anything about you on social media," Keithia begged.

I decided to let the little bitch, Meka, live another day. I knew one thing... she better not say one fucking thing to me for the rest of the night.

"Rondon must be here," Tay said curiously.

"Yeah," I replied nonchalantly.

I tried to get my breathing together before I stepped out of the truck, so I counted to twenty; I jumped out with a bold demeanor. I ignored the numerous *hey gorgeous lady* I heard from several men.

One of those skeezers in my truck hit the button that made my Range Rover talk with Plies and Akon "I Wanna Fuck You". That was my song, so it was natural for me to bob my head as I entered the gas station. I didn't glance or nod my head when I saw Rondon, Baked, J-Money, and Ruger standing in the second line.

I couldn't lie that Rondon wasn't looking good, because he did! Standing strong in an Aeropostale outfit, I felt his eyes on me. My eyes quickly strolled down to his feet and saw the black, low top Air Force Ones freshly cleaned and laced up. I saw all of this by using my peripheral vision. Yes, I was a beast with my eyes.

"That's all you gonna do is stand there like you don't know us?" Rondon asked after he was done conducting business with the cashier and walking toward me.

I didn't say anything. I just kept my eyes forward.

"Hmm, Hmm. Got your bottom grill in. Where you going?" he continued on as I pretended not to hear him.

I saw his jaws flinching, and I knew he was getting pissed. I was still on the mute mouth game. Baked and J-Money started laughing and walked out the door.

"Oh, so you really going to act like that? Okay, X. I get it. Be safe," my fine, ugly ass baby daddy voiced in a not so pleasant tone before he waltzed away from me, heading toward the entrance and exit glass door.

"I always do," I responded, as I walked up to the window and purchased the items I came there for.

All I needed was to put my vehicle on full since it was sitting on a little below half of a tank, so I knew twenty-five dollars would be good. After I gathered my things, I walked out the door to a view that made me a little warm in my heart, when I knew it shouldn't have. I saw Rondon putting the gas nozzle into my tank.

"Look at this character here," I said to myself.

Those tricks in my truck had the audacity to select "It's Yours" by J. Holiday as I was walking out the door, I shook my head. They really made me sick with that slick stuff. As I approached my truck, I didn't utter a word to Rondon while he pumped the gas. I opened the driver's door and hopped in the front seat. I knew it wasn't going to be long before those heifers stirred up something.

"Y'all two make me sick," Keithia said to Rondon and me. He laughed, and I caught a glimpse of his right dimple.

My, oh my... look away! You ain't completely over him, X, I thought.

"What you talking about, Keithia?" he questioned quizzically as I slid my seatbelt across my body and started the engine.

"The way you and X be acting toward each other lately," she breathed.

I looked in the rearview mirror at Tay, and that fool was back there shaking her head like she was disappointed in us.

"She knows I love her, and I'm not going anywhere. That's my baby she's carrying... she's gonna forever be involved in my life and vice versa," he said before walking off.

"Nih, bitch you didn't tell us that you are pregnant. Hoe, when was you going to say something?" Meka voiced excitedly as the other chimed in with congratulations.

"When the smoke cleared, I guess," I replied blankly, wanting to slap Rondon's face for bringing up the pregnancy with his messy, petty ass.

Putting the gearshift in drive, I sped off. I left the gas station in a hurry, because I knew he was going to follow me. I didn't feel like dealing with the BS tonight, but I had a little inkling between my legs.

Lord, please keep us away from each other. I have the urge to bless him with my loving, and he doesn't deserve it... Juvy does, I thought as I zoomed through the traffic light.

Within fifteen minutes, I pulled into a packed parking lot of Club Vela. The club was on wham, and I was sure to get what I came down here for. There wasn't anything special about the club, except the money that flooded through there. Well-hidden fiends frequented the club, because they knew that they would get quality dope.

As we stepped into the one level, plain Jane club, the music was pumping good, and the smell of good weed was flowing. People were conversing and dancing, and of course, the entourage was in awe. I shook my head as they started high fiving each other.

Right then, I knew they were truly some simple ass bitches, because their outfits were simple as hell... a black shirt with gray tights and some black, plain Jane Ked-like shoes, but they were from Wal-Mart. I wasn't knocking anyone that couldn't dress with name brand clothing, because before I started doing my thing in the streets, I wore non-name brand clothes, but my feet stayed in name brand shoes.

I walked up to them, stated that I had to holler at somebody, and that I would catch up with them later. As I walked toward the back of the club, I saw Mano, talking to one of his security men.

"It's so nice to see you, X," he stated with a smile on his face as he outstretched his arms.

"It's nice to see you as well, Mano. Let's get down to business, shall we?" I informed him as I motioned for us to visit his business office.

Fifteen minutes of useless chitchat and the money bag being placed in my hands. I raced out of the business room, aiming for my truck. I wanted to duck the money off so that I could enjoy my time with those crazy broads. After I completed my task of hiding my money inside of my Range Rover, I bypassed the growing admission line and aimed for the security guards. They briefly patted me before clearing me to re-enter the club.

Wanting a drink, I quickly sped past the bar and landed on the dance floor as "Dumb Dick" by Level blasted through the speakers. Getting in the center of Keithia and her crew, I started jigging to the song. I felt eyes on me, so I sneakily scanned the club to see who had their eyes on me. At the bar,

Rondon was looking at me as if he wanted to snatch me off the floor.

Chuckling to myself, I thought, *you fucked us up. You get what you get, but if you come on this damn dance floor with any mess... I will make sure this club is never open again.*

Somewhat enjoying my time out, I was missing Juvy. Wanting to chat with him, I pulled out my cell phone and texted him.

Me: I miss you, Mr. Bossy!!

With the phone in my hand, I had a smile as he replied back.

Juvian: Mr. Bossy missed his Mrs. Bossy. Do you want me to head to Clanton or post up at the condo?

The smile on my face resembled that of The Jokers as I read and responded to his text.

Me: To the condo. I'll text you the address and where you can find the key.

Juvian: Okay. Muah!

Me: Muah! Muah!

Inside of the kisses text, I included the address and where he could find the spare key. Right then, I was ready to leave, but I had a statement to make to those fuckers at the bar that thought I needed them. Stunting season was year round for me, and I was the queen of stunting and being bossed the fuck up at all times!

Chapter Sixteen

Rondon

The look on my face when I hopped on Facebook and saw that *Meka DoinJusFineBih Johnson* post that she was in Gulf Shores with X, Keithia, Tay, Pea, and Bri… I gathered Ruger, J-Money, and Baked in a flash and told them that it was time to head out the city for the weekend. I didn't tell them why I wanted to go to Gulf Shores, but they were sure to find out once I found X's ass.

Meka led me all the way to them. I already knew exactly where they were at around 10:00, because she left her location on as she was posting pics, and that caused me to pull up at the service station where they were at.

The entire way to Club Vela, I thought about X. My baby had me mesmerized from the time I saw her pull into the gas station, until she drove off in a rush to get away from me. Tonight was the night. She was going to be in my arms, running her hands through my head, and releasing all those sweet juices on my naked dick, fingers, and mouth.

It was past overdue. I hadn't been in her presence for quite some time; I was ready to make love to her, see her smile, and hear her laughter. She was going to learn that I was going to be her one and only. There wasn't going to be another nigga in her life. I wasn't hearing that BS.

As we pulled into Club Vela, Baked got excited about the snow bunnies he saw walking in. Ruger was scoping out the scene, as usual. J-Money's ass was searching for four thick broads he could smash, and I was laughing the entire time at their silly asses.

"What you gonna do once you get in this Club and see X?" Baked asked seriously.

I looked over at the nigga for a minute, and then politely responded, "Try to talk to her, and if that doesn't work, then I'm going to force her out of the club."

"Good luck, man. You know she real quick wit' them hands," J-Money stated before laughing, which caused Ruger and Baked to chuckle.

It took us thirty minutes to get in the club, and it was jumping. I scanned the scenery, scoping out for X. I saw her in the middle of the dance floor, jigging and grooving to "Dumb Dick" by Level. She swayed her ass from left to right. She looked absolutely amazing as she danced and let her hair down, as she liked to say, with the females. Her body was calling me, and it took everything in me not to run on that dance floor and snatch her up.

Out the corner of my eye, I saw Baked speed past me to talk to some chick that had been eyeing him since we walked in. Ole girl acted as if she wanted to devour my homie. He went in for a hug and damn near was lifted off the ground by the cute, thick broad. J-Money and I chuckled at that scene.

Shortly after, J-Money left me to go and holler at a blond-headed, slim chick. Ruger was off to a corner by himself, sipping and probably thinking. I was left alone, so I strolled to the bar after making a mental note to mess with Baked about damn near being swallowed whole by ol' girl. I had to get me a strong drink to get my nerves together. I really felt like walking on that dance floor and snatching X's ass up.

Within ten minutes, the fellas met up with me at the bar, we scanned the dance floor as the females were hiking that ass up and throwing it. I had to admit that they did their thing to the fast beat of the music. They had every guy in the club staring at them. Even X decided to twerk. My eyes were glued on her the entire time, and I was waiting on a nigga to get wrong.

She had me bricked, and I was anxious to give her my ten inches of strong, chocolate rod! Some chick came close to me and did a split while popping her ass. I glanced down briefly and pulled my eyes back to X who was dancing with some guy. I became pissed immediately.

I pulled out my cell phone to text her, but J-Money whispered in my ear to chill out. I strongly nodded my head while shoving my phone back into my pocket. As she danced, she was on the phone texting, and I pondered who in the hell she was texting; it sure as hell wasn't me. I was in the process of making a step for the dance floor, but Baked grabbed my arm and shook his head. Exhaling heavily, I retreated to the bar and looked on as X did her thing.

Ten more songs played before X showed her natural tail. The DJ played "That Body" by Lil Chappy, and X showed how well she knew how to maneuver every part of her body. In the hook, Lil Chappy asked the ladies to let him see them bounce, shake, and roll. My X did all that and them some... one cheek, two cheek, bust a split, and rolled her ass while doing the one cheek, two cheek... pretending to play with the pussy as she was winding her body like a tornado.

If niggas were standing behind females that were dancing, they no longer were stunting them, because X held their attention. She held her right hand up as if she was Hitler; it was the call for her goons to be close by, in case an idiot tried to get to close to her. Now, all of us looked at each other quizzically as we saw eight big, grisly looking dudes in different regions of the dance floor surround her instantly.

"What in the fuck is really going on?" Baked yelled into my ear at the same time J-Money asked the same question.

Shrugging my shoulders as I kept my eyes on the scene in front of me, I replied angrily, "I have no fucking idea!"

Growing tired of not being close to her, I became bold as fuck and rushed to the dance floor. Not having to look back, I knew that Baked, J-Money, and Ruger were not far from me. I stopped as soon as X twirled on her left foot, stopped, and looked at me as she whirled her lower waist region. She must've been doing something fantastic with that ass, because money was flying her way. After Lil Chappy's song went off, "I Can Tell" by 504 Boyz blared through the speakers, and X had a wicked smile on her face as she vibed to the song and held up three fingers.

Keithia and the bootleg crew, as I called Meka, Pea, Tay, and Bri, slid their asses around X's body as they were rapping and singing the song. The crowd resumed back to dancing, but X still had some guys star struck. They stayed close to her in case she was going to show out again. Once that song went off, they went to the side portion of the club passed the second bar to take some photos. I left the post where I stood while looking at them enjoying their time. I made sure to not let X see me while she and the ladies took pictures. I was hoping she was going to take some by herself so that I could hop in.

Two minutes later, my wish came true. I walked into the picture area and jumped in with her.

She looked at me crazily, and I held up both hands and said, "I'm just your child's father."

She nodded her head and gave the camera her bad, boss bitch pose. I swore that was the sexiest pose ever. After X and I took six more pictures, in front of everyone, I pushed her into the wall and licked her lips. She tried to push me off her, but I always made sure I brought force when I was around her—if possible. I held her head still as I pried her mouth open with my lips and tongue. She gave in, and I felt a tear grace my face. That's when she pushed me really hard and walked rapidly out of the picture section. I asked the picture man to print out all the pictures we took. He told me they would be ready in fifteen minutes. That was enough time for me to find her and explain myself.

All of her girls looked crazy at me except Keithia. I think she knew I was going to pull something. She was never surprised at my actions when X was around. I didn't have the first clue where X went, until Meka walked up to me and said she went outside and probably to her truck. As I nodded my head, I held up two thumbs and skipped out of the club. When I opened the doors, I saw her sitting in the driver's seat of her truck with her legs dangling while she roughly fumbled with her hands.

She saw me coming and yelled, "Go on about your business, Rondon! We will talk Monday. Right now, I want to enjoy my time out with my cousin and her friends."

"I'm not trying to hurt you again. I just want to talk," I told her when I was in earshot.

"X'Zeryka Nicole Toole, will you listen to me, please?" I begged, as I approached the driver's door.

"Fuck no!"

"I'm tired of this back and forth game. I'm done apologizing for how I treated you. I'm sorry that my mother got ahold of your number, and said those hurtful things! What I'm not going to do is keep apologizing for the stupid shit that I did. I'm not going to keep telling you that I want you in my life. If this is how you are going to act with me then... fuck it!" I shouted, glaring at her.

"Deuces my, nigga," she replied, looking me in the face with the "I don't give a fuck" facial expression; that shit really pissed me off because I couldn't get to her.

Her cell phone started ringing, and I didn't move a bit; I wanted to know who in the fuck was on her line, because they weren't going to get no play. She went from one hundred to zero when she said hello to whoever was on the phone. She was talking in that calm, sexy voice that she used to talk to me in, and she had the nerves to ask the next how his day was. She was giving him my attention.

Oh, hell no, I thought as I started walking toward the driver's door. I was going to snatch her up and do something nasty to her in the truck. If I couldn't get some act right politely, then I was going to steal it.

"Get the fuck off the phone!" I demanded, snatching X's phone and hanging it up.

She was ready to say something smart, but I nipped it in the bud once I grabbed her thighs, snatched her closer to me, and shoved my tongue in her mouth. She tried her damnest to fight me off her, but she failed badly. I unbuttoned her pants, and she commanded and wiggled away from me thinking that was going to stop me. I did everything in my power to make sure that my two fingers were going to reach their destination—that pussy. It took me a minute to succeed because we were in a real struggle, and I could tell that she didn't want to hit me.

Once I inserted my index and middle fingers inside of her; she cooed my name, and I blessed her with the release of pressure that was built up in her. I used the lower half of my body to spread her legs wider, so that I had better access to my pussy. I knew she wanted my fingers in her playground while she tried to fight me; I punished her with my fingers before I decided to put that mouthpiece on her. I let her know that I was the master and that I held all the keys.

"I'm tired of playing with you. This pussy is mines and only mines," I whispered against her clit as I had her in the driver's seat spread eagle with her pants and thongs down to her ankles with her legs on the roof of the truck. I didn't have time to close the truck door once I had her in that position; I was on a mission, and I didn't give a fuck who saw us.

My fingers and face drove her crazy; I ate my baby like I was starving. I ignored her cries as she begged for me to stop. I ignored the struggling of her trying to get up. I ignored it all, because deep down I knew she was done with me; I wasn't hearing that. I heard our crew coming, and I didn't give a damn since I had to please my baby. I had to let her know I wanted her more than ever.

"Rondon, get the fuck back!" she screamed-groaned as those sweet juices flooded out of her and onto my tongue. I was overly excited to lap it up.

"Man, are y'all serious?" Bri laughed upon seeing the door open and hearing X moan out in pleasure.

"I'm sorry," I stated softly to X as I tasted her.

"I hate you! If you come near me again, this baby will not know its father. Do I make myself clear?" she cried out while she released again on my tongue.

"I swear this nigga be doing the most," J-Money spoke while coughing.

I wanted everyone to know that I was gunning to be X's one and only, as she was mine. I rotated my finger around her wet pussy and sucked on X's clit until she screamed my entire name.

"Reginald Rondonnnn Martinnn!"

"Now, y'all showing out!" Pea shouted while her back was against the back hatch door.

Pulling my fingers and mouth off X, I began to laugh at the same time she said angrily, "Get up off me, and I meant what the fuck I said!"

I embarrassed her enough, so I put her legs down, put her clothes back into place, and backed away from her so that I could get myself together.

X stepped out of the truck and fixed her clothes to her likening. Then she hopped back in the truck and started the engine. I didn't say anything to her as I walked off toward my truck, since there wasn't anything to say; I spoke to her as I pleased her. Oh, the smile on my face let my partners know that I was pleased with myself.

Once Pea and her little crew got in the truck, X drove off with the speakers blasting. I knew her fingers and legs were still twitching; I had that effect on my lady. I knew for a fact she wanted the rest of me, and I was damn sure ready to drop my dick off in her.

What she didn't know was that she either was going to come to my hotel room, or I was pulling up at her condo, because I had her cell phone. Ruger was in the driver's seat, and I slid in the back besides Baked. As I pulled out X's phone, I strolled through her phone; I wanted to see who she been texting and talking to.

The moment I saw Juvian in her text thread, I opened up the text messages and grew angry as they discussed the ways they were going to taste and make each other moan.

"Ruger, pull up at the condo," I huffed angrily as I continued to read the text messages between Juvy and X.

I bet she won't be fucking or sucking that nigga again! I thought as I clenched and unclenched my fists, eager to kill that nigga!

The fellas were asking me tons of questions, and I wasn't answering a single one of them. My mind was on that ancient, black nigga that was digging up in my baby mother like it was the right thing to do. Once I was finished killing him, I had one pussy hurting to serve upon X; she was going to know that I owned everything on her, including her brain.

Ruger whipped into the condo's parking lot and parked in X's designated spot. As I hopped out of the backseat, I was gunning for the sixth floor with my partners behind me. When I hit the elevators, my cell phone chimed with Jagged Edge's song "I Gotta Be". Without having to look at my phone, I knew it was X calling.

Sliding my index finger across my phone, I spat, "Yeah."

"You got my phone, don't it, Rondon?" she asked in an agitated tone at the same time her phone started ringing in my hands.

"Nope," I lied as I arrived at the elevator and pressed the number six button.

"You is a strong, ugly face liar, nigga. I hear my phone. I want my shit back, and I'm on my way to get it. I hope you loved what you read, nigga," she yelled into the phone.

"Then come get this motherfucker and that nigga... because I'm finna kill his ass!" I told her sternly as I hung my phone up.

"Bro, what in the fuck got you so pissed off?" Baked asked soon as the elevator dinged and the door opened.

Ignoring his question and the eyes of my partners, I kept my mind on how I was going to beat Juvy down to the ground, followed by throwing his body over the balcony. My partners talked to me until the elevator doors began to open. They were halfway open when I slid my body through it and ran down the hall; in the middle of the hallway stood Juvy.

He was standing in a posture that informed me to come to a complete stop. As I did so, I studied the best way to attack him.

From behind me, Ruger stated calmly, "Are y'all going to fight or not? The shit is really crazy, Rondon."

"Shut the fuck up, Ruger. You act like you wanna be with X. Like I told you before, she's mine and mine alone," I announced angrily at him while keeping my eyes on Juvy.

"I believe she made her choice when she confirmed to me that she was going to help me raise my children, as I help her raise y'all kid. I'm not going nowhere way. So, you better get ready to see me for the rest of your natural life, nigga," Juvy barked confidently.

His statement caused me to charge toward him. What I wasn't expecting was for Baked and J-Money to run and grab ahold of me. Struggling to get free from them, I cursed and shouted.

"Get that bastard into my condo, now!" X voiced loudly as she walked in front of me with Keithia and her entourage in tow.

As I fought against Baked and J-Money, I was cursing Juvy out and telling X that she would always be mine.

No one didn't say a word until X closed the door behind her. The females took a seat on the sofas, Juvy sat at the bar, X and Ruger were standing in front of the bathroom door, and Baked and J-Money still had me in a strong hold by the refrigerator. I was talking shit, but I could back all of it up. The look on Juvy's face was blank as he glared into mine. It took X to whistle in an annoying manner for me to shut up.

"You looking like a strong ass fool, Rondon," she stated as she walked toward the bar and took a seat.

"I'm in love with you, and you are fucking another nigga. How in the hell do you think that shit makes me feel?"

"That's not my problem… that's yours. You should've known what to do in order to keep me off another man's dick, and since you didn't... well, let's just say he piqued my interest. You did the one thing that you weren't supposed to," she said calmly as she glanced at me before looking at Juvy.

"And what's that?" I interjected nastily while struggling to get loose.

"You tried to take something that didn't belong to you... you had *my* goons say that I wasn't fit to be the Queen... you and *my* other goons 'booted' me out of The Savage Clique," she laughed hysterically before cutting it short and finishing her speech, "You made me feel like I was nothing. You treated me as if I was just another piece of ass... a dumb ass at that. So, you know we will never be. If you want to co-parent, then I'm absolutely fine with that."

"Co-parent? Hell nawl, I ain't hearing shit about no co-parenting...even though we were doing a lot of co-fucking."

"Actually Rondon, we were co-fucking," she laughed before clasping her hands together and then continuing, "We weren't together. You would hem my behind up and do what you do, which caused me to do what I do. Now, this little hatred that you have toward Juvy ends immediately. The best thing you can do is leave. If you try to come for him in any type of way... let's just say I won't have to say I told you so."

Everything she said pissed me off. Here I was glaring into her face as she protected the one nigga we were supposed to have killed, when he first touched down in Alabama. I knew I should've knocked him off the first week of him being in the city.

Relaxing my body, I nodded my head and told X whatever she wanted to hear. She gazed into my eyes and quickly threw up two fingers, signaling for Baked and J-Money to let me go. When they did, I fixed my shirt and exhaled heavily. I was a master at deception, thanks to the woman I got pregnant. Strolling toward her with a pleasant smile on my face, I reached out to her. She grabbed my hands and roughly pulled me close to her.

The same growl that she gave me when I was at Capital Market, sounded from her mouth; chills ran through my body and for a minute I thought I was shaking uncontrollably. I quickly looked over at my partners, and they were standing still with a worried look upon their faces. There was never a time that Ruger looked nervous or worried, but at that moment he was both of them; therefore, I knew I should be as well.

Before I had time to plant my eyes on X, that heifer strong armed me on the floor. Juvy jumped up, and she growled nastily, "Sat yo' motherfucking ass down! I'm a woman... a boss bitch at that. I haven't turned in the card yet!"

Holding up his blackened, burnt hands, he replied as he took a seat, "Yes ma'am, Mrs. Bossy."

Focusing her attention back on me, X pulled out the beautifully special made, golden, double-bladed knife. She only pulled that out when she had important, personal information. Growling and gazing into my eyes, X was back to Chief. I didn't see her as a woman anymore; she was the devil disguised as a woman. Letting my body fall in sync with the floor, I laid on that cold, beige ceramic tile as I knew the end was near for me.

"You think you can get shit over my head, huh?" she spat in my face as she planted her nose on mine.

"Whaaa... What are you talking about?" I stammered.

"I think you know what I'm talking about Rondon."

"I promise you I don't."

"Oh, Mano, told me you reached out to him and stated that I said that he doesn't have to pay me directly. He has to go through you."

"I only told him that because I didn't want you in this street life anymore. I meant what I said about having you and our child out of harm's way," I stated honestly.

"Okay... umm, so what about the fact that you are still fucking around with Meka, and that she has a child for you... yep, the same bitch that's sitting on my sofa now," she stated before laughing and pointing at Meka.

"Chief, let me explain," I voiced defenselessly.

"Oh, now I'm Chief... is ya' scared?" she chuckled and then continued, "What about the part when Reggio cornered you last year when you and Ruger were in California, and he offered you to work for him?"

"Chief, please let me explain that one."

Shaking her head X continued talking, "What about the part when you had a threesome with Keithia and Meka six months ago? What about the fact that you got an offshore account with the same amount of money that I had in my account?"

"I don't know what you are talking about," I stated with a shaken voice.

"Oh, really?" she replied before she told Pea to hand her the envelope.

Bringing the envelope to X, Pea's hands were shaking as she tried to avoid looking at me.

"No, Pea, I want you to pull out the last six sheets and hold them in front of his face, as I tell everyone about the misdeeds of this bastard."

Doing as she was told, Pea held the papers up to my face as I skimmed through the highlighted numbers. X talked calmly but with a hint of anger. She told everyone that I switched almost five million dollars of her money to an offshore account. She also called out the dates the money was transferred from one account to the other. As she spoke on the things that were done, I was denying them all.

"Ruger, Baked, and J-Money, this nigga didn't give three fucks about y'all. He swindled the money out of the account I pay y'all monthly from," she laughed as they shook their heads and stared at me.

"That's not true, X," I defended myself while staring into each of their faces.

"Pea turn to page six," X demanded sternly.

On command, Pea did as she was commanded.

X's voice boomed through the room, "Pea, read the IP address and the physical address on that page, please."

Once again, Pea did as she was instructed to do. Tears flowing down my face, I knew I was in deep shit. There was no way I was coming back from the shit that was being held against me.

"X, baby, please listen to me... I didn't swindle the money out of your account. The other shits I did... fucking your cousin and Meka... having a baby with Meka... I did all that. Please, don't think that I would steal from you."

"That's the number one thing you shouldn't have done... was take something that didn't belong to you," she huffed before she placed the blade across my neck and began slicing the skin on my neck.

"Baby, please don't do this. I love you," I sobbed as the tears dripped down my face.

"Bitch, fuck yo' love. I'll see you in hell ... if I make it there," she laughed before Juvy hopped away from the bar, snatched her off me, and stomped me unconscious.

Chapter Seventeen

Bango

Monday, January 1, 2018

As I knocked on the door of my home, I was a mess. I had contacted X several times to see did she like the gifts that I left her. Of course, she didn't answer her phone or respond to any of the messages I sent her. While I was off in the zone thinking, my wife opened the door.

Avoiding eye contact, I said softly, "Hi."

Not responding, Taea slid to the side. When I walked in, I wasn't expecting to see my things already packed and boxed at the front door. The door closed behind me, and Taea waltzed into the kitchen. Not seeing our children in the front room, I asked her where they were.

"In my bedroom," she replied with her back facing me.

"Is it cool if I go back there with them?"

"Nope. I'll bring them to you. As you can see, all of your shit is packed," she stated calmly as she pressed buttons on the microwave.

"Aight," I voiced casually as I walked toward the sofa and took a seat.

The silence of the home almost made me want to scream. I wanted Taea to hit me or do something that would cause the silence to cease. Her being quiet was doing something to me. I cared deeply for her; I didn't want to see her in pain. Everything she's feeling and going through was because of me and my damn feelings; I guess that's what I got for not handling my feelings the right way—not asking her to marry me.

As I looked around the once vibrant and happy home, I felt that I had to break the silence. If Taea could forgive me, then I would be alright. We had to be on okay terms in order to co-parent our children. I didn't want her to be a bitter woman because of the choices I made.

"Taea, we need to talk."

The microwave dinged and she ignored me, which caused me to repeat myself.

Sighing heavily while holding her head up, she replied nastily, "Call that bitch, X, and tell her to talk to you. I'm out of fucks to give."

"Look, damn it, we have children together. Regardless of what the fuck I did... we still have to be cordial for our children. If we need to attend counselling together to make sure this works out, then I will go. However, you will not take my kids from me!" I voiced sternly as I stood and stared at her.

With two sippy cups in her hand, she spun around on her heels and mouthed in a low tone, "I will be cordial with you, Bango. Just don't expect shit else from me. I'm filing for divorce first thing in the morning."

Semi knowing that she would do that, I had already prepared myself for it.

"And I'm okay with that, Taea," I told her as she started moving away from the kitchen into the living room.

The look on her face when I told her that I was okay with her filing for divorce, damn near crippled me. She wasn't expecting me to say that, and I wasn't expecting her response. She quickly regrouped and nodded her head.

"What does that mean?" I asked, inquiring about her nodding her head.

"I guess you want to be with that bitch more than me... that you are willing to accept your best friend turned wife seeking a divorce," she hissed as tears flowed from her beautiful, brown eyes.

"I've done wrong by you, Taea. I don't expect for you to stay. Especially knowing that I slept with another woman," I explained softly.

The mentioning of me having sex with X, caused Taea to throw the babies' cups at me before running to me with balled fists.

Quickly grabbing her, I held onto her body tight as she began sob, "Why would you hurt me this way?"

For the next thirty minutes, I held Taea as she questioned what type of human being I was, and why would I hurt the one person that never brought harm to me. She kept asking me questions, and I kept ignoring them--until one required for me to answer.

"What type of person screws over a person that loves them? Huh, Bango?"

"A confused one," I stated as I held on tightly to her body while we were lying on the floor.

"I would've never done no shit like that to you."

"I know."

"Then why do it to me?"

"Because I'm one confused individual."

"No, bitch, you are a fucking savage. The streets made you a weak, pathetic savage! Now get the fuck out of my house, and don't you come back, until I say so!"

When I released her hands, she sprinted toward the children's sippy cup, which were lying in front of the sofa, followed by darting down the hallway. The entire time she was softly weeping, and saying how she hate that she married me, I shook my head.

Slowly getting up off the floor, I looked around the home that was already foreign to me. Not knowing what my next move was going to be, I gathered two large duffel bags and left.

Along the way to Snoogi's SUV, I was blank minded. Stepping out into the snowing, cold air, I didn't feel the air since I was pumped full of adrenaline. Opening the back door, I threw myself and duffel bags in.

Upon the closing of the door, Snoogi voiced lightly, "How is she?"

"A mess."

"Are you proud of yourself?" he asked as he pulled away from my home.

"Yes," I replied honestly.

"Nigga, what the fuck," he stated as he turned on the light to look at my facial expression through the rearview mirror.

"Now that everything is out in the open… I no longer have to pretend like I hate X. I am able to put her behind me and move forward. Once this is under the bridge, after numerous sessions of counseling, Taea and I will be fine," I voiced confidently while glaring into Snoogi's long, shaped face.

"Wow. You are really crazy if you think your wife isn't going to be your wife within the next six months."

"Let's just say that I know my best-friend turned wife. She's damn near close to her breaking point, but she also knows that it took a lot for me to tell her something that's hurtful and to cry while I was telling her the truth… hell I was at my breaking point. I know we will be alright."

Chapter Eighteen

Taea

Tuesday, January 2nd

I didn't get an ounce of sleep, and I wasn't tired. I was frustrated as hell. My mind was all over the place. I didn't know what to do when it came down to my marriage. I knew that I loved Bango, but not to the point that he was going to run over me; there was no way he could do the things that he has done to me without any repercussions. I was a great mother to our children and a wonderful wife. The things he has put me through were despicable and uncalled for. There were plenty of times he could've come clean about his feelings for another woman, but he didn't. He led me to believe that I was the one for him, and when it all boiled down to it I was the second-hand bitch.

As I stared at our texts that we sent each other around three o'clock this morning, I knew what I had to do. He was my heart and soul. He was the only guy that I've known on a severe intimate level. Bango was the one that was there when things were tough for me. We had matching tattoos, and a beautiful wedding band. We had two beautiful children together. We knew each other better than our own grandmother's knew us.

"Here, you go," I stated to my lawyer as I did a final once over on the divorce papers before pulling off my engagement and wedding bang.

"Are you sure you want to do this Mrs. Johnson?" the elderly, white man asked sincerely.

"It's Ms. Gresham, and I'm absolutely sure."

Nodding his head, he went through details of how the divorce process worked. Hearing him clearly, I nodded my head with a faint smile upon my face.

At the end of his speech, he asked me a series of questions, "Are you seeking alimony?"

"No."

"Are you seeking child support?"

"No."

"Are you seeking half of anything that he has?"

"No."

"Are you seeking full custody?"

"No. We can have joint custody."

"Do you think there will be a battle about you guy's home?"

"If it is... he can have it."

"Okay. I will file this right away, and send him a copy of the papers."

With the same weak smile upon my face, I replied softly, "Thank you, Mr. Wayne. Have a nice day."

"You as well."

After we shook hands, I left his beautifully decorated office, aiming for my children whom were being watched by Gonzilla.

"How did it go?" she asked as she stood and grabbed the handle of the double-seated, gray and black stroller.

Holding up my left hand, I showed off the finger without an engagement or wedding band. Gonzilla stood with nothing to say.

I chuckled lightly before saying, "Girl, let's go home and have a little fun while the children are sleeping."

"Hmm, you know I love fun," she stated while making a funny face that made me burst out in laughter.

"Thank you for being here today," I told her as we strolled toward the large, bronze elevators.

"Where else would I be? You need me now more than ever. You are going through something that can cripple a woman...

especially a woman with two children, and not to mention that you are sort of freshly married."

"Honey, I'm a strong, Black queen. The only thing that can tear me down is me. I refuse to let a man tear me down. He has hurt me one too many times."

"If you don't mind me asking, what was the final straw that made you sign those papers, because last night you said that you weren't going to sign them. You were going to give y'all space," she asked curiously.

At the same time the elevator dinged, I handed her my phone with Bango and my text thread pulled up, I stated firmly as we waltzed inside of the large elevator, "Read... all of it."

Me: What were you really thinking about, Bango, when you violated our vows?

My Hubby: What were the feelings that I possessed for her? Whether she was just a nut or a person that I actually loved being around. Was there still passion left between her and I, which was destroyed by two meddling people?

Me: Did you ever find the answer?

My Hubby: Yeah.

Me: What was it?

My Hubby: There was still love there. However, it is strained.

Me: When you slept with her, did you treat her body like you did mine?

My Hubby: No.

Me: Did you fuck her without a condom?

My Hubby: Yes.

Me: Were you drunk?

My Hubby: No.

Me: On Christmas, were you thinking about her?

My Hubby: Yes.

Me: Did you purchase a pair of gold Giuseppe stilettos, an expensive beautiful black sundress, a special made gold necklace, a four-hundred-dollar spa gift card, a customized I love you Hallmark Christmas card, and had a gold pendant with the names of Bango and X, inside of it?

My Hubby: Yes.

My Hubby: She has had a rough life, and I felt bad that we have family that care about us. I wanted to let her know that no matter what she was okay in my book. That her and I were in a cool place, and that I felt her pain that she has been struggling with since we were younger.

My Hubby: Can we go to counseling... I don't want this to cripple us as parents. I don't want my mistakes to fall on our children. I love them, Taea. You may not believe it, but I love you also.

Me: You made love to her... that's why you didn't treat her body like you did mine... lol. You've probably never done my body the way you've done hers. You bought her all of that expensive shit for Christmas, and you are going to tell me that you didn't treat her body like mine. You wanted me to believe that you fucked and left... nawl, you stayed... you ate pussy, fingered the pussy, tongued kissed her in the mouth, put your dick in her raw and all... YOU MADE LOVE TO ANOTHER WOMAN WHILE BEING MARRIED TO ME!

My Hubby: I love you, Taea.

Gonzilla handed me my phone, and the tears were streaming down my face as I read along with her.

"I hate him, Gonzilla... I fucking hate him. How could he do this to me? The one female that always had his back. How could he make me the second bitch? He didn't have that much respect for me to tell me how he felt for the next? How am I supposed to look at him now? We have two beautiful children," I cried as she opened her arms and I ran into them.

"It's going to be alright. You and those beautiful babies you and him have created are going to be alright. Yes, it hurts like shit now, but I am going to see you through. Take as much time as you need to let your heart mend. You deserve more than what you have been giving."

Pulling out of her arms, I wiped my face and nose with the Kleenex that I had in my purse. The elevator doors opened, and I retreated toward the back of my kid's stroller. Learning to hold my head up high through the rough times, I did just that as I flounced out of my lawyers building. I knew, without a doubt, that I would be able to recover from the hurtful blow brought on by the man that stood before God and our families, confessing happily that he would honor and love me for the rest of his days.

As Gonzilla and I stepped into the lovely, bright but snowy day, I was able to grin and thank God for showing me what type of man I was married to. I should've known that I couldn't turn a hoe into a husband!

Chapter Nineteen

X

After we left Gulf Shores early Monday morning, I decided that Juvy and I should be staying at my safe house; therefore, when we arrived in Montgomery County, I made sure to hop on Highway 80. Juvy protested about being in the country, but I quickly told him that we weren't staying long.

I knew he hated being in a heavily wooded area; that was the sole reason for me making up my mind to go there. It was a great way of getting Juvy to love the country life. I wanted him to experience how much freedom he had in the country versus in the city. How refreshing it was to wake up and not have people staring you in the face, soon as you walked out of the door.

Escaping to my favorite area of Alabama, I prayed it would aid Juvy in loving it as much as I did. If he was cool with living in the heavily wooded area on the weekends, I would be fine with that. After all, he was a city boy; I was willing to compromise with him.

I loved my little single family, three-bedroom house with two full baths; the master bedroom had a garden tub so big that I would get lost in it. The yard decorations and planting of flowers were done by myself. Gardening was a relaxing hobby that I took a big interest in, thanks to my grandmother. She taught me how to take care of the flowers and weeds, so that they wouldn't have my yard looking a mess. The grass was perfectly green with no spots of brown.

On the patio, I had it setup with nice, floral patio furniture, a tan porch swing, and several plants hanging from the ceiling. The backyard and back porch were decorated with the same types of yard fixtures just different furniture and type of wood. Inside of my little safe-haven, I had it remodeled with the latest modern black furniture, appliances, and different electronic devices.

I loved to read books in my spare time, so of course I had a black, trimmed in gold bookcase that housed different genre books. Every part of my safe-haven was fully furnished. When I started to get more items than I intended, I would get rid of the things that I didn't want. I meant I wasn't going to have a house full of unnecessary furniture.

Fifteen miles away from my safe-haven, tucked comfortably in the middle of the woods sat my lab; a well put together nice-sized, dark brown shed was the place where I made the magically delicious narcotics, so I've heard the fiends call it. There was no furniture in my lab. From the time I waltzed through the door, I would be standing on my feet in full protective gear, whipping, mixing, and making quality product.

As I stood in a casual brown dress and black ankle socks, thinking while looking into the direction of my laboratory, I felt light kisses on my neck. Turning around on my heels to face Juvy, I smiled before planting a kiss on his lips.

"Are you going to miss your lab?" he breathed against my forehead.

"Not at all. I have led this life for a long time, and now it's time to give it all up."

"Ruger, Baked, and J-Money stated that they wanted to talk with you, X. I think you should hear them out," he voiced softly while looking into my eyes.

"I know. They texted me and I responded for them to come by around four o'clock. Soooo, I think you need to get the grill ready. I'm in the mood for barbecue ribs, chicken, and grilled asparagus," I stated happily as I batted my perfectly curled eyelashes.

Chuckling lightly, he replied, "Sounds good to me. I knew you were hinting at barbecue today by the smell of the fridge. You got that mug on wham. You seasoned those three slabs of ribs well, Mrs. Bossy."

"Why thank you, Mr. Bossy," I announced excitedly while smiling.

We became silent as we enjoyed the chirping of the birds, the chilly air, and the brightly shining rays from the sun. Of course, the weather in the south did a complete three-sixty overnight, and the temperature was back in the low sixties.

As we continued to enjoy each other quietness and bodies, Juvy broke the silence by asking me, "Have Rondon tried to reach out to you?"

"No," I responded honestly.

"Do you think he will be a problem in the future?"

"No. He knows what I'm capable of doing."

"You better hope he does, because this time you won't be there to stop me from killing him," Juvy voiced firmly but delicately as he gazed into my eyes.

"I'm sure he wants to be a part of this child's life."

"And I'm okay with that… as long as he don't meddle where his nose don't belong."

Looking at the time off Juvy's watch, I realized that it was time to get the feast on the road.

"Mr. Bossy, it's two-thirty... so let's get this cooking thing on the road."

"I'm with it. It's too early to fire up the grill, but I can help you out in the kitchen," he said coolly as he lifted me off the ground, while I wrapped my legs around his waist.

"I would love that, but you know what I would love more, Mr. Bossy?"

"What's that?" he questioned as he opened the black screen door.

"Some of Mr. Bossy's loving," I cooed in his ear.

"You ain't said nothing but a thing," he voiced passionately in the crook of my neck as he outstretched my body on the kitchen table.

***

After we ate, all of us retreated to the back porch to talk. I felt relaxed and had a positive outlook on things. I informed the guys that I did recover the money from Rondon's hidden Switerzland back account, and that I transferred their monthly earnings last night. Baked told us that DB's family was looking for him.

Of course I busted out laughing, followed by saying, "They are going to have one helluva time looking for him. What did you tell them, Baked?"

"That I haven't seen him in months. I fed them some more bullshit about him hanging out with some chick from Canada," he voiced casually as he rolled a blunt.

"Cool," I responded at the same time I thought of one more thing that I had to do before I ceased my old life.

"What do we do now?" J-Money voiced curiously.

Turning my head to look Josh 'J-Money' Harris into his medium-sized, dark brown eyes, I softly replied, "Anything but be a snitch. Live a normal life if you want, or link up with another illegal drug dealer, or start your own organization. It's completely up to y'all."

J-Money responding without words; instead, he used the nodding of his round head for acknowledgment. As he continued to nod his head, I chuckled because he was imitating a bobble head. That six-foot-one, dark-skinned, goofy, tight-end built nigga, I was truly going to miss. He was laid back and willing to give his shirt off his back for you. He was very smart, and for the life of me, I didn't know why he chose to hid it.

"Ruger, what are you going to do?" Baked asked my trusted advisor.

Sighing heavily, Ruger responded, "Well, Marvin 'Baked' Russell, I'm leaving the game alone with X'Zeryka. My goal is complete. I made sure that she is alive and well."

The laughter that roared out of my mouth wasn't because of what Ruger said, it was the way that Ruger stated Baked's first name.

"Don't y'all start no shit about my name, nih," Baked laughed, while firing up his blunt at the same time he hopped up from the chair and waltzed down the beige steps.

"Ruger?" I called his name softly as the guys stopped laughing.

"Yes?"

"I've been observing you for years…," I began to say before his chuckling cutting me off.

"I knew that it was going to come. Now, X'Zeryka, this here I have to hear, and I will be completely honest with you. Shoot at it," he told me as he laid back in the light brown, cherry wood chair and gave me his full attention.

"When I was sixteen, I picked you for a reason to be on my team. It was something about your swagger that had me interested in being around you more. When I was under Tyke, I always admired how you moved in silence and barely talked to others in the organization. There was some type of mystery to you, but there was also pain in you. I'm just thinking about how long we've been together in this game, and how much each of us has really missed out in life as far as making a family of our own. What's your story?" I asked curiously as I folded my legs.

Ruger bit down on his bottom lip before he spoke. I wondered what was causing him to think carefully before he said a word.

"Right before, I left to go to basic training in 2001, I lost my mom, dad, two sisters, my baby brother, and three-month old son to a senseless murder by two stupid ass niggas that wanted to be in a gang. Word circulated around Chicago about who did it, and I murdered those boys and their families along with whoever was in the house, including the little baby that was sleeping in the crib, followed by me setting the house on fire. With that type of shit on my conscious, I didn't want a family, and I'm still having troubles with being in a committed relationship for fear of karma," Ruger confessed as he stared into my soul. None of us uttered a word, so he continued, "And actually, I requested to be under your wing since you reminded me of my sister Janet; she was three years younger than me. I knew I was going to protect you at all costs, since I wasn't around to protect her. I've killed for you; for the simple fact that I didn't want any harm coming toward your way. I love you like a sister and I always will."

Words didn't form right in my head, thus I kept my mouth closed. The hurt he must've felt for his family and the baby that he killed was heartfelt. I couldn't imagine being in his position; he had so much to deal with, all the while making himself suffer. We didn't break eye contact, even when I got up and walked to the liquor cabinet. I poured everyone a shot of Moonshine in a clear plastic cup, handed the fellas one, and I watched them toss it back, while I turned up the water bottle.

"I don't regret killing their families, X'Zeryka. I regret not being there for mine," he replied honestly as I looked at him. I nodded my head, followed by biting down on my bottom lip.

"Hell, I wouldn't have felt any remorse for their families either. Hell, I guess because I'm a fucking savage," J-Money voiced casually at the same time Baked agreed with him. Before I knew it, all of us were agreeing with J-Money's statement.

The night went by slowly as we enjoyed each other's company. Once the ten o'clock news aired, we made sure to watch it. The newscaster started commenting on the set of fires that took place in different areas of Alabama. The cities he mentioned had the fellas looking at me as I held a huge grin on my face.

"You, set all the safe houses on fire?" Ruger asked before chuckling.

"Indeed," I replied as our eyes landed on the old, white male inquiring on the details of Darnell 'DB' Brown, as DB's picture flashed across the screen.

Squinting my eyes, I yelled, "Time to do a real quick clean up. Y'all we got one more assignment to do."

"Time to make sure no one speaks of seeing him with The Savage Clique," J-Money, Baked, Juvy, and Ruger stated before we hopped up and peeled to our whips.

Chapter Twenty

Juvy

X and I made a run toward Huntsville and the surrounding areas, while the other guys had their designated spots they had to cover. She made sure to call her peoples in different states, informing them not to say a piping word about DB and who could know him.

It was well after midnight before X, and I returned to her country home. We showered, followed by talking and eating a late-night snack. Our chemistry was amazing. I loved being around her; I knew without a doubt that she would be my wife. Everything about her was intriguing, and I knew it would take me a lifetime to get to know her; thus me, telling her a truth of my own.

"X?" I stated calmly as I pulled her on top of me.

"Yes?" she voiced lowly but seductively.

"I have a confession to make?" I confessed as I held her beautiful face close to mine.

"Would your confession be... that you blackmailed my child's father?" she laughed before shaking her head.

"Yep," I voiced lowly while gently rubbing her back.

Laughing lightly, she announced while rubbing my nipples, "I already knew that. I have cameras in all of their houses. I saw when you snuck in his home and was held hostage at his laptop. I also heard you say, 'I bet this fuck nigga gonna get out of the way now'."

With a shocked look upon my face, I had to know why she went alone with the act.

"Why did you continue to frame him along with me?"

"Because I wanted that character out of the way. Since, you already set the trap... I just finished it off for you; thus, having the guys fall out with him. They think he stole money from me, and I want to keep it just like that. I don't want to deal with him on that level. I need him scared of me."

"Is it okay if I tell you that I adore you, X'Zeryka?" I exhaled as I slid my mouth toward hers.

"Is it okay if I only want you and you only, Juvian? Is it okay if I tell you that I'm feeling you more than I can express, Juvian? Is it okay if I tell you that I know without a doubt that within two to three months I will be telling you that I'm in love with you?"

"Hell yes. All that shit okay, guh," I voiced happily as I flipped her onto her back and began to leave a trail of kisses from her mouth, followed by my mouth holding onto the small, delicate bud of her pink, moist, delicious tasting spot.

"I'm all yours, Juvian King," she cooed.

"X'Zeryka Toole, I'll forever be yours."

Chapter Twenty-One

X

April 2018

The air was so much better once I left the game. I smiled, slept, had wonderful orgasms more, and had a different but better outlook on life. I finally was able to breath. I was free of Bango's, Tony's, and my uncle's hold on my heart. The feeling of leaving the streets behind unscathed, with a peace of mind, was worth every criminal activity that I committed to receive being criminal free.

I didn't have the urge to manufacture or sell drugs; I didn't have the thoughts in my head to go back to the street life. I did yearn for Ruger, but I knew he was in a better place. He was living in California with a female that he'd been sneaking around and seeing. Baked and J-Money decided that they wanted to leave the streets to live a normal life with their family and friends. Rondon was back in Iowa with Meka by his side. Baked, J-Money, Ruger, and I conversed on the phone every day via Skype. Nothing changed about those fools.

I heard through the grapevine that Bango and Taea were no longer married. Upon me hearing that, I reached out to him. Giving him my apologies, he accepted and told me that he would always love me. My family was the same, still on that bullshit; so of course, I left their ass on that level. Keithia and I didn't talk anymore, and I was okay with that. I finally visited Silky Snakes family and his final resting place—the goons were with me. Reggio's charred body was found miles away in his severely burned SUV three months ago, and I didn't ask Juvy any questions. I already knew who was behind that.

Juvy and I were living in the countryside of Marbury, Alabama with his two children. They were beautiful, well-mannered children, and I loved them as if they were my own. Bryson was just like Juvy, and Taylor was exceptional. She loved to paint and fix on cars. So, off the bat, she and I hit it off. She was extremely smart, but she didn't like to read books. I had to put her on The Boxcar Children books, and before I knew it she was asking to visit libraries followed by going to Books-A-Million.

Each day I looked into their happy, smiling faces, I knew that things would be alright for us... mostly myself. The more

I was in Juvy's arm, I knew without a doubt that I was ready to be Mrs. Juvian King.

"Hey, baby, are you okay? How's our little princess doing in there?" Juvy asked, smiling while rubbing on my little basketball of a stomach.

"Yes, I am okay, and this little busy body is up and moving around," I stated as I stood up to kiss him. I was twenty-four weeks pregnant, and I enjoyed the blessing that was bestowed upon me.

Scooping me into his arms, Juvy began to twirl me as I laughed while the sun was beating down on our bodies. Our children joined in on the fun and started spinning themselves around. I finally had the feeling of real love. I had a man that wanted me, just as much as I wanted him. I didn't have to worry about the different women, late night calls and texts, disappearing acts, or anything disrespectful.

There was nothing else that I could wish for. I had my happily ever after, with no worries in my brain!

About the Author

TN Jones was born in Montgomery, Alabama, but raised in Prattville, Alabama. She currently resides in Montgomery, Alabama with her daughter. Growing up, TN Jones always had a passion for reading and writing, which led her to writing short stories.

In 2015, TN Jones began working on her first book, *Disloyal: Revenge of a Broken Heart*, which was previously titled, *Passionate Betrayals*.

TN Jones does not have a set genre she writes in. She will write in the following genres: Women's fiction, Mystery/Suspense, Urban fiction, Dark Erotica/Erotica, and Urban/Interracial Paranormal.

Published by TN Jones: *Disloyal: Revenge of a Broken Heart, Disloyal 2-3: A Woman's Revenge, A Sucka in Love for a Thug, If You'll Give Me Your Heart 1-2, By Any Means: Going Against the Grain 1-2, The Sins of Love: Finessing the Enemies 1-2,* and *Caught Up In a D-Boy's Illest Love 1-3*.

Upcoming novels by TN Jones: *The Sins of Love 3: Finessing the Enemies, Is This Your Man, Sis: Side Piece Chronicles,* & *I Now Pronounce You, Mr. and Mrs. Thug.*

Thank you for reading the final installment of *Choosing To Love A Lady Thug*. Please leave an honest review under the book title on Amazon's page.

For future book details, please visit any of the following links below:

Amazon Author page:
https://www.amazon.com/tnjones666

Facebook: https://www.facebook.com/novelisttnjones/

Goodreads:
https://www.goodreads.com/author/show/14918893.TN_Jones:

Google+:
https://www.plus.google.com/u/1/communities/115057649956960897339

Instagram: https://www.instagram.com/tnjones666

Twitter: https://twitter.com/TNHarris6.

You are welcome to email her: tnjones666@gmail.com; as well as chat with her daily in her Facebook group, **It's Just Me...TN Jones**.

CPSIA information can be obtained
at www.ICGtesting.com
Printed in the USA
LVHW091737191219
641092LV00002B/192/P

9 781796 471939